Ever been torn between two lovers? That's Ricky Comparetto's problem.

It's 1995, and Ricky is making his very first trip across the pond with his best friend. Ricky, hungry for love and looking for it in all the wrong places, finds it in the beach city of Brighton. His new love has the curious name of Walt Whitman and is also an American, which only serves to make him sexier and more intriguing. By the time Walt and Ricky part, promises are made for a reunion in Boston.

But the course of true love never runs smoothly. In Chicago Ricky almost immediately falls in love again. Tom Green is a sexy blue-collar beast with the kindest heart Ricky has ever run across.

What's he to do? With a visit to the East Coast on the horizon and a new love blossoming in Ricky's home of Chicago, Ricky truly is torn.

I0590595

TORN

Rick R. Reed

A NineStar Press Publication

www.ninestarpress.com

Torn

Printed in the USA

Print ISBN: 978-1-64890-041-9

First Edition, June, 2020
Originally Published in May, 2019

Also available in eBook, ISBN: 978-1-64890-040-2

Warning: This book contains sexually explicit content, which may only be suitable for mature readers, and death of a prominent character.

For Sukie

If you love two people at the same time, choose the second one, because if you really loved the first one you wouldn't have fallen for the second.

—Johnny Depp

It is not time or opportunity that is to determine intimacy; it is disposition alone. Seven years would be insufficient to make some people acquainted with each other, and seven days are more than enough for others.

—Jane Austen, *Sense and Sensibility*

True love is not a hide and seek game: in true love, both lovers seek each other.

—Michael Bassey Johnson

Prologue

Present Day

I'm going to tell you how this story ends, but not with whom. That's a fair promise to make, isn't it?

So, yes, you'll get your happy-ever-after ending—if there truly is such a thing—you just won't be privy to *all* the details. Unless you read on...

Almost twenty-five years ago, I was thirty-five years old and privileged to cross the pond to merry old England for the very first time. I was finally able to say I'd traveled internationally by the grace of my best friend, a writer of boys' adventure stories with the improbable name of Lord Boutros BinBin (no, he was not an actual Lord; he told me once he simply had parents who were "quirky" and "creative," also known as "free spirits"). He wrote under the much plainer moniker Beryl Kensit.

At that time, and during that trip, I was also blessed to fall head over heels in love with a gorgeous, kind, and sensitive man I met at twilight on the streets of the beachside city of Brighton. He ticked every box on my imagined list for the perfect lover—exotically handsome, spiritual, artistic, amazing in bed, and...I could actually hold a conversation with him. Our silences were okay too, comfortable. We launched into a passionate affair and promised that we'd meet again.

But the course of true love, as they say, never did run smooth. Ain't it the truth?

I returned home from those two weeks with a satchel full of memories, a sexually transmitted infection, and the knowledge that I'd found true love.

But then, only a week or two after settling back into my little apartment in the Rogers Park neighborhood of Chicago, I found myself falling head over heels in love *again*—this time with a salt-of-the-earth, charming, and sweet man from the South Side. He was nothing like I ever imagined I would be compatible with—our tastes, educational background, intelligence, and cultural awareness made us like creatures from two different planets—yet somehow the magic, the spark, was there.

How would I reconcile the two? Whom would I choose? Could things ever end satisfactorily when, as in Mary MacGregor's song, you're "Torn Between Two Lovers"?

Read on, my friend, read on...and discover how the head won out over the heart.

Or was it the other way around?

Chapter One

1995

It was the cheapest flight we could find. Air India, round trip, O'Hare to Heathrow, around seven hundred bucks. We snatched up the fare because my best friend, Boutros BinBin, was homesick and wanted to show me his homeland, "the place that made me who I am." If you know Boutros, you know this is a scary thought. And yet I still wanted to go.

We snatched up our tickets because we were both sick of Chicago, dreading the humid summer we knew was in store, and because I had done about every guy on the North Side.

Joke. Now Boutros, hush. And stop rolling your eyes!

We'd do London (and EuroPride). We'd do Brighton (Boutros called the seaside town the San Francisco of England because it was *so* gay—in a good way). We'd do Boutros's ancient hometown, Bath. Honestly, one of us would *do* just about any attractive male within the age range of eighteen to, oh, sixty-five—but the latter part was always negotiable. In the dark, a hard dick is a hard dick.

Or maybe I'd find Mr. Right. "You'll find a hundred Mr. Right Nows if I know you," Boutros said. Boutros could always see through me like I was made from glass. It was this attribute that I both loved and hated about my best friend—and probably what drew us together when we'd met a couple of years before at a gay writers' group called the Newtown Writers, in Chicago. I was drawn to his sense of humor, and he was appalled by the Daisy Dukes I wore to the first meeting.

Just a few short years later, we were both summarily thrown out of the writers' group. Boutros said it was because we were the only two who'd been published, and I argued that it was because we appeared at a meeting at his house wearing nothing but a smile. Gay men! They're always trying to get you naked, and then, when they succeed, they get offended!

We agreed to lick our wounds over coffee. Compounding the pain of being ousted from the writers' group, I had recently ended a relationship. Boutros lent a sympathetic ear to my man troubles, which were then all about my indolent, smart, perpetually stoned, and job-challenged boyfriend, Henry, whose life revolved around marijuana—growing it and smoking it morning, noon, and night. I wondered what it was he needed to escape. When I asked Boutros, he told me, "Probably because he can't stand waking up sober next to that face. And I can't blame him." Only Boutros could say such things to me, knowing I would somehow interpret them as demonstrations of love and caring. When we finally broke up after Henry had quit yet another job that was way beneath him, I cut ties.

And yet, I was devastated. Boutros led me through mourning the end of my first gay love with a firm hand, a lot of sarcasm, and a willingness to listen while I rambled on and on into the phone, wondering if I'd done the right thing. After all, Henry could be sweet, although he'd never admit it. On the day Henry moved out (while I was at work—a concept foreign to him), he left the CD player on and Whitney Houston's "I Will Always Love You" playing on infinite loop. Even though I knew Boutros was probably appalled by the sappiness of this gesture, he listened as I choked out words of devastation through sobs, and demonstrated admirable restraint when he could have cut me down to pathetic size with a couple of *bon mots*. Support like his, coming at a crucial time, often cements two people together.

It did us.

So when Boutros proposed we jet off across the pond together, I was beyond thrilled. Even though I knew I couldn't afford it on my catalog copywriter salary, which barely paid my rent, going to Europe, especially England, had always been my dream. I'd grown up with a pen pal from the West Midlands and had developed a keen interest in the place from her long letters describing Cannock Chase and the little Staffordshire village in which she lived. Perhaps I could see her, too, while I was there. It would be our first meeting in person.

Boutros convinced me to clean out my bank account for the trip by saying that once we got there, we could stay with friends and family wherever we went. All we'd have to pay for was food (fish and chips!) and drinks (Guinness!). We'd get around via the tube, and for longer distances, we'd take advantage of England's very user-friendly trains that went just about everywhere.

I desperately needed a break from my boring job and from nursing my broken heart (even if I was the one who technically broke it), so I was on board.

Well, actually, I was on board right that very moment, Boutros next to me. We were on a double-decker plane that was enormous, much bigger than anything I'd ever flown on—not that I'd flown much, just a handful of flights between Chicago and Pittsburgh, Pennsylvania, which had the closest airport to my hometown of East Liverpool, Ohio.

The flight attendants, all women, wore saris. The plane was filled mostly with eastern Indians. Heathrow was a layover for them, not a destination, as this flight continued on to New Delhi.

"Ah, the sweet smell of curry is in the air," Boutros whispered, leaning close to my ear.

"Hush." I looked around, praying no one had heard him. I got his sense of humor—which involved saying a lot of things simply for their shock value—but I doubt that anyone else on the plane would.

I already felt as though I'd stepped into another world. I couldn't wait to get to our destination and see what adventures were in store.

One of the flight attendants came around pushing a trolley. On it were small Styrofoam cups and full-size bottles of whiskey.

"Would you like?" The dark-haired woman smiled at Boutros and me, gesturing toward the bottles and cups.

Indian custom? I shrugged. What the hell? "Yes, please. One for me, and one for my friend here." I leaned back a little so she could see Boutros in the middle seat. I doubted she could miss him, though, dressed as he was in palazzo pants with a yellow-and-purple paisley pattern, and a white muslin peasant shirt. His black hair stood up in a multitude of directions, and his mustache, waxed, stuck out so far, he could make the truthful claim that one could see the mustache from behind him. The goatee below the mustache was just beginning to gray. His earring and nose ring were connected by a dangling silver chain. He liked to say his face was "done up like a Christmas tree."

Sometimes I wondered if people even saw me when I stood next to him.

"One?" Boutros scoffed. "Amateur. Could we have two?"

She nodded, smiling, and poured us each two shots of whiskey. She handed them over, and we both quickly downed the first and then handed the cups back to her. Boutros belched and said, "Check back on us, would you?"

The flight attendant's smile didn't waver. Serenely, she moved on to the next row to ply the whole plane, I presumed, with strong spirits.

Boutros reached for his leather backpack, which he'd stored under the seat in front of him. "Surprise! I've got a little something here that will help shorten the flight, if you know what I mean." He grinned mischievously as he groped around in the bag's outer compartment. He brought out a prescription bottle and shook it. A couple of pills rattled.

"Morphine, sweetie, from when I had that cyst out in hospital. Remember? I punched that nun when they started cutting before the anesthetic set in." He leaned close, rubbing up against my shoulder. "I saved these two just for you and me, darling."

"You're too good to me. They say time is the most thoughtful gift, but I beg to differ. I say it's drugs." I returned the shoulder nudge, then held out my hand like a beggar.

We popped the morphine, washing it down with our second shot of whiskey. The unvoiced plan, of course, was that we would sleep on the overnight transatlantic flight, arriving in London the next morning refreshed and ready to begin our sightseeing after dropping our stuff off at Boutros's friend Trevor's place in Westminster.

Maybe I was too excited to sleep, but even after a third shot of whiskey *and* morphine, I was still wide-awake for the full eight-hour flight. And perhaps my excitement was contagious, because Boutros couldn't catch a wink either. We watched our flight's progress on a screen on the back of the seats in front of us. I thought, *Hurry, hurry.*

If anything, the drugs and alcohol had the curious effect of making us even more bright-eyed and bushy-tailed than either of us usually were. After trying fitfully—and desperately—to sleep, fluffing the thin and starchy pillows our flight attendant had given us, we passed the night talking about what we'd see and do, following the vivid colors and subtitles of the inflight movie, *Raja*, which was, from what I could gather from the subtitles, a romance about a young man reuniting with the woman he was supposed to marry years earlier. We ate the meals the airline offered—chicken tikka masala and basmati rice for me and saag paneer and rice for him. Even though it was Indian food, which Boutros and I both adored, it was airline food...and thus barely edible. Fortunately, they brought out the complimentary whiskey cart again near the end of the flight.

And, at around 10:00 a.m. London time, we touched down on the runway at Heathrow International Airport.

Chapter Two

We took the tube from the airport to the St. James's Park stop in Westminster. Walking out of the tube station, I had the nagging sensation that this was all a dream. I was sure I'd wake up at any moment in my double bed in my one bedroom in Rogers Park, my black-and-white cat, AJ, pawing at me and demanding his breakfast. The Chicago L would thunder by just outside my bedroom window, throwing up sparks from the tracks. The sun would throw slats on the old hardwood floors.

Except now there was this almost surreal aspect to everything—the bustling crowd on the sidewalk, the curdled-milk-white sky, the British accents I heard in snatches of conversation, and the simple sense of history that was everywhere I looked.

My God, I'm really here!

I realized in an instant how *young* my homeland is.

We lugged our bags along the sidewalk as we searched for Boutros's friend Trevor's apartment. Along the way, we passed through St. James's Park and then on into narrow streets, some with open-air vendors selling fruit, baked goods, and touristy souvenirs. I made a mental note to get myself, at some point, a Mind the Gap T-shirt with the iconic London subway system logo.

We saw things that required me to simply halt our passage and stare—these were postcards come to life. Westminster Abbey, the houses of Parliament (and Big

Ben!), the buildings clustered along the Thames. Everywhere I looked was a piece of living history. I knew I should be worn out, but my heart raced, and I felt energy that should come from a good night's rest but was, in reality, the result of the adrenaline my overexcited system was pumping out.

We passed a couple of teenage kids, a boy and a girl, camped out on the sidewalk in front of, ironically, a bank. They were surrounded by fast-food wrappers, an open guitar case, and a couple of rolled-up sleeping bags. The boy had a mohawk and wore tight, pegged jeans paired with a provocatively ripped Ramones T-shirt. The girl's turquoise cotton-candy hair, pulled up in a sort of beehive, framed her elfin face. She wore a plaid school uniform skirt, white blouse, ripped fishnets, and cherry Doc Martens.

Boutros leaned down to add a couple of pound coins to their guitar case. There was already a mishmash of currency there—coins mostly, along with some bills.

He eyed the kids. "I want you to promise me you'll spend that money on drugs."

They giggled but eyed him a little suspiciously.

We walked on, the morning glaringly bright, the wind warm, bordering on hot.

"Are we there yet?" I asked. The tiniest bit of fatigue was beginning to filter in. I spied it out of the corner of my mental eye, waiting to be acknowledged. I knew its patience was running out.

"Almost. It's just up the way, I believe." Boutros cast a gaze at me. "This is cool."

"What?"

"I'm seeing this through *your* eyes. It makes it all new again. And exciting."

I nodded. The fatigue was coming into plainer view. My bag, an old leather duffel that once belonged to my dad, was gaining weight with every step I took. My black nylon backpack was mysteriously getting heavier too.

We finally wound up outside an old redbrick courtyard building. We were a stone's throw from the St. James's tube station. The building was in the heart of everything one imagines when one thinks of London—close to the Thames and all the iconic landmarks, dripping in British charm and grandeur. Something occurred to me. "Your friend Trevor must have a great job to be able to afford a place here."

Boutros shrugged. "I'm not sure what he's got on at the moment. Anyway, it's a council flat, so he doesn't pay much."

We rang Trevor's buzzer.

I watched through the leaded glass window as a wide figure clambered down the stairs. The latch was thrown, the door opened wide, and Trevor stood there to greet us. He was a big man—both in terms of height and width—with a shock of thinning blond hair and skin so pale I wondered if he could qualify as a legitimate albino. But then I looked into his dark brown eyes and realized he was simply pasty. Color rose to his cheeks as he eyed us both. He didn't hesitate to grab Boutros in a bear hug, squeezing him so tight Boutros gasped and pushed him away. "Get off me!" he snapped.

Trevor laughed, and the old cliché of being fat and jolly rose up in my head. "And who's this tasty morsel?" He gave me a once-over, wrapping up his inspection with a lascivious wink. *Uh-oh*, I thought. *Boutros told me Trevor's flat is only a one bedroom. Will I be expected to share a bed with our host? There's no such thing as a free lunch, or in this case, free accommodations in a posh part of London. I will do what I must for the cause of cheap lodging, but I hope I don't have to. Nice as Trevor seems, I don't think he's quite my type.*

But Lord knows I'd never ruled anyone out before for not being my type! I would say I'd been egalitarian in my past choice of bed partners. Boutros would say I was simply an undiscerning slut. "Any cock'll do!" he'd once quipped.

God, I adored him.

Trevor extended a hand; we shook. I peered into his dark eyes, smiling. "I'm Ricky Comparetto. Boutros's friend. From the States," I babbled, discovering that suddenly I was more than a wee bit nervous.

Trevor laughed, a big gruff sound, appropriately eyeing me like I was some sort of lunatic. He mimicked what I'd said, making it sound harsh and flat—what I suppose my American—Chicago in particular—accent sounded like to him.

But then a warm smile lit up his face. "Welcome, Ricky from the States!" He turned a little to gesture toward the stairs, which I could now see were carpeted in some kind of faded pink floral pattern. Cabbage roses, maybe? At the first landing, there was a lovely stained glass window in hues of violet, cobalt, and yellow. Simple squares and rectangles of varying sizes. "My castle is your castle. Come on in."

He turned to head up the stairs, stopping to grin at Boutros. "You can come too."

"Of course I can, my dear. My presence can only lighten up this dreary shithole."

They both chuckled.

We headed up the stairs.

The flat was small. Cramped kitchen with a clothes-drying rack perched above the sink. On it, two pairs of jeans and a black T-shirt. Miniscule counter with a microwave and electric kettle. Appliances that looked miniaturized compared to their American cousins.

The main living area was fairly ample, the walls painted a cheerful yellow and bordered by white baseboards and crown molding. Scattered around was what looked like thrift-store furniture, brightened by throws in almost eye-hurting shades of turquoise and orange. A little black here and there calmed the color riot. A bay window looked out onto the courtyard.

Trevor led us into the cramped bedroom. A full-size walnut bed with a chenille bedspread, neatly made, graced the room. The only other furniture was a nightstand next to the bed and a small black lacquered dresser. A cut-glass lamp stood on the nightstand, and beside it was a bottle of lube.

"Didn't this belong to your mum?" Boutros ran his hand along the white chenille fabric. "Weren't you conceived on it, during a shore leave?" He picked up the lube and considered it, set it back down. "I believe that belonged to your mum, too, didn't it? They always talked shit about how 'dry' she was. I assumed it was because of her sense of humor." Boutros snorted.

Trevor rolled his eyes and ignored him. "You two will be in here, so just throw your bags down and make yourselves at home." He paused, one forefinger at his lips. "You lot are okay with sharing a bed, right?" He raised one of his eyebrows, making me notice for the first time that he had a pair—they were so pale as to be almost translucent.

"Oh, we're not a couple," I blurted out, lest Trevor had the wrong idea.

Trevor squeezed my shoulder. "Darling, I didn't think that for a moment. You? With this ancient queen? Never!" He shivered.

"He'd be lucky to have me, Trevor. I've seen some of the trolls he's taken home from the bars. Believe me, I'd be a huge step up." He eyed me, grinning. "We'll be fine. Thank you."

The bed was calling to me. The overnight flight and the jaunt through the busy streets of London had finally caught up, demanding restitution.

I plopped down on the bed and tried for my best British accent. "I rather fancy a nap. Do you chaps mind?"

Boutros's upper lip rose in a sneer. "I could just kill him."

"Me too," Trevor agreed.

"Go on and have a nap. I have a night out planned for us. You'll need your rest," Trevor said to me, and then to Boutros, "Come on, then. Fancy a spot of tea?"

Boutros followed. "I'll be mother."

The last thing I remember was the white door, thick with many, many coats of paint, closing.

Chapter Three

Much later, I found myself wandering the streets of London near New Scotland Yard, searching through its labyrinthine corridors for Trevor's building. In the quiet darkness of London's wee small hours, it seemed the world had paused to take a breath. Again, a feeling of things being surreal overcame me; I wondered if I'd ever find my way back to Boutros again, or if I'd be doomed to wander endlessly through this curving warren of streets.

It was maybe three o'clock in the morning, and Westminster felt almost like a movie set, perhaps something dystopian, where the main character wakes to find the world empty. The light of Big Ben shone in the distance, but I had no idea how to get back to Trevor's.

I was too exhausted to panic, however, even though I felt like a rat in a maze, a charming, historic maze, but a maze nonetheless. Looking back, I recall that I felt serene, strange as that is to remember.

I had just decided to see if I could find a park bench or curb to lie down on—to await morning's light and new clarity to get back to my friends—when I discovered that there was such a thing as a bobby, the Brits' word for a patrolman on foot. This bobby, who was dressed all in black with a tall hat adorned with a shield, and I appeared to be the only ones about, other than the black cabs that passed by stealthily, similar to the one that had deposited me in a place I'd believed was close to Trevor's.

I approached the bobby and told him, a little abashed, that I was lost. I supplied him with the name of the street I sought and, for good measure, what Trevor's building looked like.

He nodded, all business. "You need to cross the Thames"—he pointed that way—"and then make your way back in the opposite direction from where you were going. You're not far."

I thanked him, but his directions simply didn't *feel* right. I didn't want to argue with him, and I certainly didn't want to believe he was fucking with me, so I didn't question him. I may have been lost, but I wasn't *that* lost. I let him continue on his rounds. I stood still, not wanting him to see me continue on what he'd most likely perceive as my misguided path. *Why'd you bother asking him if you weren't going to listen?* I wondered but had no good answer for myself.

I plopped down on a bench to ponder what I should do. I supposed that, with morning's light, Boutros would be worried (or worse, would believe I'd shacked up with yet another man) and come looking.

I questioned my decision to part from Boutros and Trevor earlier in the evening, when the gay club we were drinking at closed its doors way too early for me. I mean, really, eleven o'clock? And this was "swingin'" London? Trevor suggested I go to an "after-hours" club called the Brick. He told me it was a no-holds-barred kind of place. Or was it "no-holes-barred"? Whatever. The idea of the "Felliniesque" club, as Trevor described it, appealed to me.

So I went, met a few nice boys, and ended the evening by being showered with come in a cloakroom, courtesy of one half of a couple I'd met who were visiting London from Liverpool.

I thought it would be easy to get home because Trevor's building was within walking distance of New Scotland Yard, which is where I told my cabbie to drop me.

I hadn't counted on streets that curved, and ended and began with no rhyme or reason. I hadn't counted on the buildings and streets all looking so alike.

I should have.

After a while, I got up from the bench and started wandering again. And then I stopped...and sighed with relief. Just ahead was one of those iconic red phone booths you might imagine when you think of London—or *Doctor Who*.

"Oh thank God," I whispered, making my way to the booth. I groped in my pocket, hoping the receipt upon which Trevor had written his phone number earlier was still there. *What if it isn't?* I thought, the panic already causing my pulse rate to quicken despite my fatigue, the copious amounts of alcohol I'd imbibed, and the two orgasms I'd had at the Brick.

But my hand curled around the little slip of paper, and I brought it out and squinted at the scrawled number in the wan light. I lifted the phone off the hook, deposited a mystifying array of coins that I hoped would be enough, and dialed.

Trevor answered, voice heavy with sleep.

I told him my problem and described where I was, along with the cross streets nearby.

He didn't seem fazed, for which I was grateful. "Hang on, sweetie. I'll be right there." He disconnected before I could say anything else.

I left the phone booth and sat down on a curb. I regarded the crescent moon above for only the shortest of times. Trevor appeared before me, like an angel, within a matter of fewer than five minutes.

I didn't have much to say, other than to express my gratitude...and embarrassment.

His building turned out to be around the next corner.

Chapter Four

The next day arrived too soon. I nursed a brutal hangover. Naturally, Boutros reveled in it, going all Baby Jane on me and snapping up the window blinds to let the early morning sun shine in, screamingly bright. Wasn't London supposed to be gray and foggy? He might as well be banging a fry pan with a serving spoon. It would be just as annoying. He eyed me on the bed, squinting. Hands on his hips, he threw his head back and fairly roared with laughter. If ever I'd suspected the man was a lunatic, the time was now.

"Pace yourself, Ricky. We don't want to have the really big fun all at once." He'd already dressed—dowdy for him—in a pair of jeans and a Cockney Rebel T-shirt, bright yellow with red lettering. He'd rolled up the sleeves of the tee to show off the Anubis tattoo he'd gotten shortly before we left Chicago.

I got up on my elbows and then rubbed the sleep out of my eyes. "What? You think this is funny?" I sighed and slumped back down. "Could you shut those damn blinds? Please? I need a few more hours of sleep—I'm beggin', sweetie." There was a little man stationed behind my eyes, hammering away in there with an ice pick. My stomach churned—I could both hear it *and* feel it.

"I will not." He yanked the sheet and bedspread off, hurling them to the foot of the bed. I lay there in all my naked glory, early morning wood pointed up toward my chin despite the fact that I felt like shit.

"Dreaming of me again?" he smirked. His gaze lingered a little too long on my erection. I rolled over, recognizing the potential for awkwardness in this situation.

I reached down to yank the covers back up, causing the pain in my head to spike. "You wish." I rolled over and closed my eyes, hoping the act would shut him out of my life completely.

He pulled the covers off again, a little less forcefully this time. "Come on, then. We don't have time for this. It's almost half past eleven."

"So?" I pulled the covers up again.

And he pulled them down again, this time leaving them in a puddle on the floor. "You have just enough time for a quick bath. We have a train to catch."

My legs curled up toward my chest in a modest fetal position. Into the pillow, I mumbled, "What are you talking about? What train?" I hazarded a look up at him. I had to squint because the sun shone so brightly behind him that it made him a silhouette. He reminded me of a scene from one of those alien movies I was once so fond of.

"*Tsk.* How many times do we have to go over our itinerary? We're off to Brighton today, in a little more than two hours' time. Remember? The train leaves at two from Victoria."

My alcohol-muddled brain vaguely remembered making this plan at the vegetarian Pakistani restaurant we went to last night. I thought I might have even been excited about it. Now, all I wanted to do was sleep. Forever...

Boutros turned to leave the room. "Up to you. You can lie there all day. But I'm off to Brighton. I've booked us a room at a gay bed and breakfast there, up from the boardwalk and near the nude beach. It's summer, and the city will be crawling with horny homosexuals. But if you need your sleep, I'll see you when I return to London."

"Crawling with horny homosexuals" had the desired effect on my libidinous psyche. I managed to swing my legs over the edge of the bed. I looked down at my dick, still pointing heavenward. I gave it a little slap. "I wish I had your stamina, your zest for living, your *joie de vivre*," I said to it.

I managed to stand and hobble, the sheet wrapped around me toga style, to the bathroom. Somehow I avoided peeing on the ceiling. I washed my hands, splashed some water on my face. When I caught sight of myself in the mirror above the sink, I despaired. I looked as though I'd aged ten years in a single night, with bags and heavy circles under my eyes. Were my partying days over? That look in the mirror also revealed there was no shower, only a tub. Why? In this day and age, why on earth wouldn't a person have a shower?

Ours is not to question why, ours is just to bathe, and bathe, and bathe...

I sat on the edge of the tub, turned the handles, and regulated the water temperature.

I was just thinking how lovely it would feel to sink into the steaming water when Boutros called from outside the door. "Trevor made us a proper English fry-up! Hurry, before it gets cold. Eggs, beans, tomato, mushrooms, and blood sausage!"

My stomach jolted at the mention of blood sausage. I hurled into the toilet bowl. I shut off the taps and looked longingly at the water. *Maybe a little grease in my system will perk me up.* Wrapping the sheet around myself, I opened the bathroom door.

*

Not all that much later, we were pulling out of Victoria Station, Brighton-bound. The train was crowded this Friday morning with revelers off to the seaside for a weekend holiday. Many of the revelers were gay boys like me. I couldn't help engaging in some subtle eye contact with the best-looking ones.

"Oh, for Christ's sake," Boutros said. He blew out a big sigh.

"What?" I batted my eyelashes at him.

"You've never been here."

"So?"

He gestured toward the window. "The gorgeous English countryside is rushing by, and all you can do is look at the men." He sneered. "So typical. You could be on the gallows, waiting for your execution, and you'd be winking and blowing kisses at the observers."

"As long as they were cute," I responded, quite reasonably, I thought.

For his sake, I glanced out the window. Row upon row of the same buildings stood banked along a hillside. Yes, it was different from America—from Chicago, certainly—but come on, there was nothing all that thrilling about the view, either. Just a lot of what Trevor had called "suburban council flats" before we left for the train station that morning.

The men, on the other hand, were, for the most part, choice. "Look," I said to Boutros. "Mind your own business. You admire what you want about merry old England, and I'll do the same."

He pursed his lips and rolled his eyes before swiveling away from me to stare out the window.

My hangover had vanished, chased away by the fry-up we had for breakfast, which, I had to admit, was pretty amazing. Even the blood sausage, which wasn't at all bloody but was very dark in appearance—not all that appetizing, but tasty anyway.

And my libido had been awakened by the multitude of gorgeous men on the train. I never did get to take care of the morning wood, and now Mr. Lower Head had risen up again, curious and hungry, demanding attention.

I caught the eye of a cute black guy across the aisle. He looked to be in his early twenties, with freckled skin, pale brown eyes that I'd call a sort of umber, and close-cropped red hair. When he smiled, he revealed a wide gap between his front teeth. Now, I know he might have sounded closer to Howdy Doody than Idris Elba, but trust me, he oozed sexuality. His compact body was all tight muscle, with broad shoulders, huge guns, and a package that promised a full meal rather than a snack. All of this was shown off admirably by the tight jean shorts he wore and his orange ribbed tank top. I threw him a wink, which caused him to stand, like magic.

He paused, hand on the back of the seat before him, before ending his meaningful stare to head toward the back of the train.

The rear of the train held the dining car and the men's room.

Either one would provide me with a satisfactory dining experience.

Boutros turned around in his seat. He'd witnessed the whole eye-to-eye exchange. He cocked his head as I began to rise from my own seat.

"I need to use the bathroom," I whispered, leaning toward him.

"Of course you do. From the looks of things, I imagine that in a few minutes time, the bathroom won't be the only thing getting 'used.'"

I grinned and stepped into the aisle. "Fingers crossed."

Then I hurried away to follow. Luckily, Mr. Tight Bod wasn't yet out of view. I stayed a few steps behind as he navigated the train's narrow passageway. I prayed for three things—that he wasn't heading for the dining car, that he was indeed bound for the men's room, and that the men's room would be empty, with the bonus of a secure lock. I had a narrow passageway of my own I hoped he'd soon be navigating!

I breathed a sigh of relief as I spied the men's room door open just a tad, indicating it wasn't occupied. I breathed a sigh of lust when he, after glancing pointedly back at me, slipped inside. I listened for the sound of a latch being thrown and heard nothing.

Good.

I glanced around and waited for a nun to pass by. She smelled of malt vinegar, My Sin perfume, and judgment. I watched her broad black-and-white expanse until it disappeared into the dining car. Then I took one more look around, thrilled to see not a single soul in the corridor.

I crossed myself and ducked inside.

He waited, slouched against the tiny sink. He'd already undone the top two buttons on his fly. I sidled up to him, our eyes communicating so much more than our mouths ever could. My own bald hunger reflected back to me out of those incredible umber eyes.

I started to open my mouth to ask his name, at the very least, but as soon as I parted my lips, his mouth was on mine with almost feral need. He thrust his tongue inside, and I sucked on it. His face appeared smooth but was delightfully sandpaper-y against my skin. I was glad I hadn't bothered shaving since a day or two before we left so he'd have the same sensation.

We clutched each other close, grinding our crotches together—making me afraid I'd come in my pants. The moment, of necessity, was all about urgency, all about blind, demanding hunger. This wasn't an opportunity to take one's time, not when a conductor might come knocking at the door at any moment.

He stopped kissing me abruptly and whirled me around, reaching from behind to undo my fly and yank my shorts down around my ankles. *Oh God, is he gonna fuck me right here?* As much as I wanted it, I wasn't at all sure this was the right time or place, exciting as the idea was. Common sense questions intruded:

Does he have a condom?

Am I clean enough down there?

Will such vigorous activity attract the unwanted attention of passersby?

People walked to and fro outside the door. As I mentioned, this was a pretty full train.

But then he dropped to his knees, pressed his face close, and buried the tongue that had been in my mouth in my ass. I rose up on my toes, the warm sensation almost like an electric shock, and then I eased back down into it.

I was in heaven, seventh heaven. I leaned forward to give him easier access. I reached back and spread my cheeks for his talented tongue, swallowing the moan that ached to emerge. At least for now, I could manage to keep quiet. But if he kept those wonderful ministrations up—and let me tell you, the guy was an absolute maestro with his tongue—I didn't know that I could stay *mum*—and we were not talking the Queen Mother there! A huge moan was lodged in the back of my throat, held in place by clenched teeth. It was positively quivering for release.

In a daze of lust, I wondered if this would go anywhere else. Perhaps he would expect the same from me? Perhaps he'd replace that tongue with his cock? And would I be able to say no to that? My heart rate slowed a little as I realized *this* is what he wanted—so who was I to stop him? He nuzzled his face deeper into my ass, licking and munching away like a starving man. He gripped my hips to pull me even closer, which wasn't even possible.

My dick stood at attention, jerking and oozing precome.

It wouldn't be long.

I turned my head to whisper over my shoulder. "I'm close, buddy. Is that what you want?"

He made this kind of drawn-out *uuugh* sound that I took as a yes. His tongue ramped up its speed and intensity, and reality disappeared around me. I was no longer on a train in England, heading toward the seaside. I was in paradise.

I shot, the white jets of come spurting up and out of me like Old Faithful. They hit the metal wall and ran down.

He turned me, feverish, so he could lap up what was still coming out.

"*Leche*," he whispered. "Mmm..."

Ah, so he's a Spanish speaker, an odd thought to have at that moment.

Also at that moment, someone jostled the door. Then banged on it once, twice, three times. A male voice, with a bit of what I heard as a Cockney dialect, cried out, "Come on, then. You've been in there ten fucking minutes. There are other people on the train, you know."

I looked down at—oh God, I didn't even know his name—and he looked back up, his tongue still at the head of my cock. A line of come dribbled down his cheek. I reached to scoop it up and feed it to him.

Only then did I give him a look of panic.

He moved back and stood, taking a step or two toward the door. His shorts were down, and there was his cock, at least eight inches, pointing heavenward. I lamented that I would not have time to attend to it. *What a waste!*

I grabbed some very rough, single-ply toilet paper and wiped away the few drops of "leche" he hadn't managed to consume, then tossed it in the commode. I flushed.

He opened the door, and I figure he knew as well as I did there was no graceful way to exit. It's not like I could hide somewhere. He was out and into the passageway almost as fast as I could blink.

Smiling in what I know was the very definition of sheepish, I followed, edging by the man outside the door, who eyed me, snickering.

It was a good thing he was dressed in a pair of black Spandex short shorts, combat boots, and a tank top that proclaimed, "I'm not queer, but twenty quid is twenty quid."

He was cute, all blond hair, green eyes, and muscles. I tossed him a wink just for the hell of it, one that I hoped said, "I'll catch up to you later."

I hurried back to my seat, face burning, in spite of the positive outcome of our close call.

Boutros eyed me. "Mission accomplished? Did he drain you? Or did you drain him?"

I shook my head. "If I told you, you wouldn't believe me. We almost got caught! Thank God—" I stopped when I realized Boutros wasn't listening. Nor was he looking at me.

He was looking at the guy across the aisle—my men's room lover.

And the guy was looking back at Boutros and smiling very flirtatiously.

The nerve! What a fickle heart!

Well, I reasoned, *I guess he didn't get the chance to be satisfied.*

I leaned back in my seat, telling myself I had no control over things. I certainly had no right to the jealousy I felt. I watched the same scene Boutros had watched only minutes ago occur—only this time, it was Boutros following the guy to the rear of the train.

Maybe the guy in the Spandex is still back there, and they'll have a three-way! And then the nun will come in and get on her knees... Get a grip, Ricky!

I shut my eyes and tried not to think about Boutros enjoying what I just had. There was something oddly incestuous about it, which made me a little queasy. I concentrated on the gentle rocking motion of the train.

And waited.

In what seemed like less than five minutes, Boutros stepped over me to get to his window seat.

"You have about you something of the cat that ate the canary."

He gave me a look that was both mysterious and mischievous.

"He was good, wasn't he?"

"Ohh..." Boutros drew out the word, then closed his eyes for a moment in what I assume was remembered bliss. "He's a lovely kisser."

Chapter Five

Boutros left me to see if our room was ready at the bed and breakfast he'd booked. He'd stayed there before and was acquainted with the gay couple who owned it—an Englishman and an Egyptian, whom Boutros said were forever fighting. "They're Martha and George—Brit style," referring to Edward Albee's dysfunctional couple at the center of *Who's Afraid of Virginia Woolf?*

I was soon to find out why they were so combative.

The place they ran was, Boutros claimed, a "dump." "But it's cheap and our room has a shower in it." This was the only place we'd be staying where we'd actually have to pay for lodging.

"And a toilet and sink, too, I presume?"

"No. Those are down the hall. We share them with whatever other Eurotrash is staying there," Boutros grinned. "Knowing you, you'll be sitting in the loo all day, door unlocked, pants around your ankles, hoping to meet someone nice."

"One never knows," I'd shot back. "Wouldn't that be a lovely how-did-you-meet story to tell our grandchildren one day? I can just picture them—all wide-eyed with a case of the warm fuzzies." There was no use feigning propriety where Boutros was concerned.

I really didn't expect the place to be a dump. I knew already how Boutros's mind worked. He was merely lowering my expectations so I'd be thrilled when I saw the place, but I didn't tell him that. Boutros was a contradiction—a gruff exterior barely concealing a soft heart. "I'm not romantic at all," he was forever proclaiming. "I'm cold."

Anyway, at least I hoped I was interpreting his agenda—and his mindset—correctly. One never knew with him. I also hoped that our bed and breakfast would be one of the charming cream-colored Victorian homes I'd seen lining the streets of Brighton. They were so common that I thought it was almost a sure thing we'd wind up in one.

So I found myself wandering alone, filled with the expectancy that anything could happen. I was in a foreign country where hardly a soul knew me, the sun was bright, the temperatures were unseasonably hot, and there was the salt smell in the air, unique to seaside towns.

I meandered for a while, confident, because Boutros had written out directions for me from the shoreline, so that if I got lost, all I had to do was go to the beach and use his directions to get to the B&B. Neither of us wanted a repeat of my first night in London.

As I walked along the busiest street in the center of Brighton, aptly named Queen's Road, I sensed someone looking at me—intently. I searched the gazes of the crowd around me but saw no one. Traffic was busy, both of the foot and motorized type.

It wasn't until I peered more closely into the backup of traffic that I saw *him*. I don't know if I'm taking literary license or if I truly did experience a unique sensation. My heart gave a little lurch. The hustle and bustle all around me dimmed for a moment. The world became silent.

He was stopped at a light, driving a little economy car of some sort unique to England, or at least Europe, and had lowered his sunglasses down his nose a bit to: one, let me know he was checking me out and two, reveal a pair of amazing pale brown irises. He grinned and raised his eyebrows, flirting from fifty feet away, even in traffic. One corner of his mouth rose in a disarming and mischievous grin.

I smiled shyly and coquettishly ran a suggestive hand over my crotch. Me, I was all about the subtlety. ("All class, you are," I heard Boutros proclaiming.)

He laughed. The light changed. Someone behind him honked, and he moved on.

What a friendly town. That little thirty-second love affair bodes well for me. I walked on, picturing him. Even though I'd only seen him for seconds, his long reddish-brown hair, a little beyond shoulder length, and matching mustache, combined with those penetrating eyes, made a lasting impression. Even if I never saw him again—and I doubted I would—something had passed between us in those moments, something that held a kind of promise.

Ah, you're making too much of a quick cruise!

I'd seen very little of his body, so my imagination filled it in—beefy, with long legs, broad shoulders, and hell, while I was at it, a big, uncut dick lying along one bare thigh. Hey, a girl can dream.

I moved on and soon wandered down to the seaside. The Brighton Pier stretched out before me, rising up from the shimmering blue waters of the Atlantic. It looked both dreamlike and touristy, with its big domed arcade, Ferris wheel, and other rides standing in the forefront of the electric blue of the sky. Endless rows of concessions promised teeth-rotting and waist-expanding delights—candy apples and cotton candy, or what Boutros referred to as candy floss. Distant music reached my ears. It would be fitting if the music was from a calliope or something befitting the historic look of the old pier, but reality stepped in, as it had a nasty habit of doing. The music was, in actuality, the Outhere Brothers with their dance club hit "Don't Stop (Wiggle Wiggle)." It seemed wrong but oddly fitting. Time and musical tastes march on, despite charming Victorian facades.

And the music did make me want to wiggle...a little bit.

I kept walking, imagining coming back here at night. I figured the pier must be even more magical then. I could visualize getting lost in the play of light and shadow, the music, the rush of the sea toward the shore.

I moved on toward the beachfront and found a bench. I plopped down. My feet were beginning to ache. Boutros had told me that there were days one could see all the way across the English Channel to France. I peered over the shimmering blue expanse, trying to see land, but either my eyes weren't strong enough or France was lost in shimmering heat waves and the slight haze hanging in the air.

Still, it was a lovely view, and it calmed me. The sun's reflection on the water sparkled like diamonds. The heat was intense and surprising, almost tropical. This was not what I expected from England.

I was glad for this moment alone. It felt a bit like the quiet before the storm. I came to the sudden realization that my life had been a whole lot of storm lately. I felt both younger than my thirty-some years and older too. I was a little jaded, and if I were being completely honest with myself, a bit immature.

I'd been married to a woman (a college sweetheart), and although I could honestly admit our three years together had been happy, they were still a lie because I had yet to accept myself for who I was—a gay man. Neither bisexual, as I first claimed when I came out of the closet, nor "confused," as one of a pair of therapists I went to had told me. The years I wore a mask were marred by discontent and wondering if anyone really loved me. How could they when no one knew the real me? The people in my life—family, friends—only saw an image of myself I cast upon the world. They never saw the man hiding in the shadows, yearning to be freed from the chains of his hidden life.

The funny thing, I now thought, was who I'd hidden from the most. And that would be me. I laughed a little when I remembered that first shrink telling me that I only longed for good friendships with men since I'd had such a contentious relationship with my father when I was growing up. "Find a good male friend," he'd urged me. Once I did that, his line of thinking went, my desire to get down and dirty with any number of blonds, brunets, and redheads would beat a hasty retreat.

The truth was, the more I resisted my urges and yearnings, the stronger they became. The old saw "what you resist, persists" was very true.

And here I was still growing up (I wondered if *that* process ever truly came to a close). The friendships with men that worked best for me these days were those where we enjoyed hobbies together, like fellatio and anal sex. Those are wholesome guy pastimes, right? Like watching football—and a hell of a lot more fun. Hey, I like a *deep* friendship with a man.

That therapist was deluding not only me, but himself. After lots of reflection, I knew I was born gay—and it wasn't the result of being damaged or maladjusted. My family may have been dysfunctional, like everyone else's I knew, but they'd never be able to make the grand and magical claim that they made me gay.

No one had the power to do that.

Boutros had said there was a nude beach around here somewhere, but I'd yet to stumble across it. He'd also promised that across the road from the nude beach was a desolate area of bushes and natural nooks and crannies that were a hotbed of gay sexual activity.

Perhaps a morning stroll would be in order? A blow job in the bushes as the sun rose? How romantic!

As I gazed out at the sea, I realized I was right where I needed to be and at the right time. My journey to self-acceptance had been marred by shame, guilt, self-loathing, and denial. Heartache. But I'd needed to pass through those stages to find the young man I sat with here today, along this beautiful seashore where the sun dazzled and shimmered on the water.

I realized this young man was simply what he was—a good person. I had healthy appetites, sure, but they were, in my opinion, God-given. If handled right (and maybe, if I could find it, with a bit of dignity), they could be a source of lifelong joy. And there was absolutely nothing wrong with that.

Being surrounded by others of my kind calmed me, validated my existence, made me sure I had nothing to be ashamed of. Nothing to celebrate, either. I was one variation on the human theme, here to complete my journey of love and discovery. Unique—just like everyone else.

Here I was in this town Boutros had called the British San Francisco because of its large gay population and its tourists—who were also of the same-sex persuasion. I was surrounded by men like me, who loved other men like me. And it felt as warm and comforting as the sun shining down upon my head.

Being here was a real vacation, a departure, in more ways than one, from what I'd always known. Boutros had told me, in one of his more serious moments, that this trip across the sea could be broadening in ways I couldn't imagine.

I knew something earth-shattering could happen—even if it was only a fleeting moment that shook the Earth. I had a portent that what would happen on this trip might affect me profoundly for the rest of my life.

All the faces of strangers passing me right now were smiling, laughing, chattering, cares tossed effortlessly on the summer breeze. Boutros would say this was on account of them being "on holiday." But for me this was a special moment in time, a revelation of the joy always there for us beneath the surface. These happy people were merely leaning into it.

Whatever the reason, I felt like Tony in *West Side Story* when he sings about something coming, something good. Who knew?

My dirty mind veered off in the direction of "coming" and "good," and I told myself it was time to get to the bed and breakfast. Undoubtedly, Boutros would wonder where I was. Or he would assume I'd picked up a trick on the street or in one of the public men's rooms that lined the beach. (Boutros called them cottages and said that they, too, promised seamy and semeny sexual delights that would make my head spin and possibly, later on, my dick burn when I peed.) Yeah, he'd probably imagine me bent over in some toilet stall, trying to hold in my moans, since he thought so highly of me.

Still I wanted to see this "dump" we were staying in and begin our "holiday" in earnest. Or in Ernest, should I run into him in one of Brighton's many gay bars. In Ernest, Phil, Clive, Trevor, Julian—the possibilities were simply endless and mind-boggling.

I set off for the B&B with an optimistic grin on my face.

*

"Mr. BinBin has already taken care of everything. Your room is all prepared for your comfort." He pointed toward the curving mahogany staircase behind us. "Climb the stairs to the third floor, make a left, and go all the way down the hall. Yours is the last on the right. I believe Mr. BinBin is waiting."

The front-desk clerk, who I assumed was one half of the Egyptian/Brit couple who owned the place, handed over a key. His hand was very soft. He reminded me very much of Mr. Humphries from the old British situation comedy *Are You Being Served?*. He was a little younger, and his hair hadn't yet turned completely gray, but he had the same fussy manner about him. He wore a lavender linen shirt with a paisley scarf in shades of yellow and purple tucked in around his collar. A diamond stud winked at me from his left earlobe. I could imagine him, decades ago, as a young twink in the Swinging Sixties, pairing that lavender shirt with striped bell bottoms and a wide white belt.

"Breakfast commences promptly at 7:00 a.m. and ends around tennish. But if you're famished, I'd advise you to get to the dining room on the early side. Regrettably, we sometimes run out of things, like rashers of bacon." He beamed at me. "Get here early, and you'll enjoy a full English." He smiled and cocked his head; then he dismissed me. "Now, I would imagine you'd like to get settled in."

I nodded and thanked him. I wanted to ask what his definition of "full English" was, but I could leave it until the morning, when I could see with my very own eyes.

If I'm not up until the crack of dawn with some gorgeous hunk...

I lifted my duffel bag and headed toward the staircase.

When I reached our door, I heard a scuffling noise inside. The creaking of bed springs. Laughter. Furious whispering. Now, a more considerate friend might have been discreet, dropping his bag outside the door and heading back downstairs for, perhaps, a cuppa. But that wasn't me. And it wouldn't have been Boutros either, if the tables, or in this case, the bed, had been turned. I grinned, raised my hand, and rewarded the old door with a resounding chorus of blows, hard enough to make it quiver in its frame. I snickered.

All went silent for a moment, and then there was that same frantic whispering. I wished for a glass to hold to the door so I could hear what was being said.

I'd raised my hand to knock once more when the door swung open. A swarthy type greeted me, all wide dark brown eyes, disheveled black hair, and a forefinger stuck in his mouth. He pulled it out with a popping sound akin to a champagne cork being released. He winked and regarded his finger and said, "Mmm...curry." And then he brushed past me to hurry down the stairs.

For once in his life, Boutros lay prone—and, I assume, helpless—on the bed. His jeans were around his ankles and his shocking yellow T-shirt was bunched up to just below his armpits. He eyed me over one shoulder.

"Thank you," he whispered.

"For what?" I sauntered into the room and dropped my bag on the floor. I stood and watched as Boutros sat up and readjusted his clothing. He lit a cigarette.

"That man is very forceful. He was about to take my honor."

I turned to look at "that man" as he hurried down the stairs. Then I crossed the room to close the door. "Are you okay?"

Boutros laughed, scooching up so he could lean against the headboard. "Well, I would have been, if you hadn't come along. That was one of our hosts, by the way. Anwar something-or-other."

I nodded, understanding Boutros's earlier reference to the owners fighting like George and Martha in *Who's Afraid of Virginia Woolf?* but unable to imagine the swarthy Egyptian paired with the effete host I'd just met.

Curry? I shuddered.

I did a quick survey of our room. Was nothing ever updated in this country? Flocked red wallpaper, dusty rose carpeting, and a cherry dresser and chest of drawers filled the cramped space and tore a page out of a 1930s history book. The furniture was dwarfed by the freestanding fiberglass shower in the corner.

"What was he talking about? Curry?"

Boutros rolled his eyes. "He'd just had his finger up my arse, stupid."

"Ugh." I shook my head and joined him on the bed. "Leave it to me to ask all the silly questions." I nudged Boutros with one shoulder. "I'm up for a nap. But then what will you feel like for dinner?"

"I fancy a curry," he said, and we both collapsed simultaneously into giggles and each other's arms.

*

After our nap, which was long and delicious, much like the cock I'd glimpsed aboard the train here, we took a detour down to the waterfront before heading out in search of sustenance, Indian or otherwise.

Boutros said, "I want to show you the nude beach. It's just along the way, down from the regular, clothed beach. There's a sign that tells you it's nude."

"I would imagine there are other signposts that clue you in as well," I said as we hurried toward the seashore.

Boutros picked up on my lascivious tone and said, "Don't get your hopes up, dear boy. Or anything else for that matter. My experience with nude beaches is that they do not always attract the people who should be running around au naturel, if you know what I mean."

When we got to the nude beach, after slogging through the sand of the "regular" public beach, I discovered what Boutros meant.

Since it was getting on toward dusk and the sky was a shimmering shade of slate blue, the nude beach was sparsely populated. A couple of older men lounged near the water's edge. They'd laid out a striped blanket, tucking its corners into the sand to make it wind resistant, and reclined on it, their hands loosely linked. Their bodies were lobster-red from the day's unrelenting sun, and their hairy bellies stood up like twin peaks. Sunglasses covered their eyes, even though the sun was close to setting, and I wondered if they were asleep.

Spread out along the sand were several more naked folks. A family with a male toddler and a little girl with dark hair who appeared to be eight or nine years old. The children frolicked in the surf, building a sand castle. A young hetero couple lay in each other's arms across two beach blankets. He was hot and handsome—his olive complexion and hirsute musculature (even down to his snowy white ass) made me think "Italian" and "*paisano*." He lay on his stomach next to his much fairer girlfriend, who was all masses of red hair, freckles, and huge tits. I wondered if he was lying on his belly to conceal his excitement at being so near to his beloved.

An assortment of folks, perhaps a couple dozen in all, of varying ages, races, and orientations (I guessed) spread out across the wide expanse of pebbles. The white ones all had one thing in common—they looked like they'd been on the beach for a while and were all sunburned. I shuddered as I wondered what a sunburned willie would feel like.

Ouch.

Boutros led me down to the sand. "If you squint, you can just see France." He gestured toward the sea.

I scrunched up my eyes obligingly, taking in the wide expanse of blue-gray waters, capped with white waves, and nodded. "Sure can. Amazing," I said. I didn't really see anything beyond miles and miles of water, but I didn't want to disappoint him.

We'd both shed our clothes back by the sign that marked the beginning of the nude beach. I'd had the presence of mind to bring my backpack along to stow them in. It felt liberating being naked—and I wasn't at all awkward around Boutros. We'd seen each other naked plenty of times in the past, so there were no shocking revelations. Boutros was Boutros—skinny, pasty, but with a huge dick that more than made up for anything one might consider a deficit. And the twinkle in his eye as he romped across the sand gave him a kind of magical charm.

The sky was at that ethereal hour when it was still light but darkness was just around the corner. The day's bright sun was but a memory.

Grinning at me, Boutros carefully wrote my name with his toe in the sand.

I was touched by his sweetness. And maybe just a little in love with him, and I told him so, using a line cadged from one of my favorite movies, *Steel Magnolias*. "I love you like I love my luggage."

He shook his head, about, I believe, to add a heart to the "Ricky" he'd written in the sand when he stubbed his toe, hard, on a partially submerged rock.

His face scrunched up in agony, and he stumbled.

And love or no love, all I could do was laugh as a big wave crashed around my ankles.

Chapter Six

We'd dined on fried plaice (a kind of whitefish that's absolutely delicious), chips, and mushy peas in a little restaurant opposite the nude beach. The restaurant was tiny, painted bright yellow, with a big picture window that looked out to the sea. When I asked for an iced tea, they looked at me as though I was crazy. They brought me a Coke with no ice instead. But the fish was delicious, moist and flaky, with an airy, crunchy batter. The chips were a revelation—outside the Weiner's Circle in Chicago, I'd never had fries so delicious, thick-cut with a crispy exterior and velvety interior. I drowned them in malt vinegar, which made them even better. I even liked the mushy peas—which tasted like something my mom would have poured out of a can back when I was a kid in Ohio. Little did she know, all she needed to do to make them authentic Brit food was mash them up with a fork.

At the end of our meal, Boutros confessed he wasn't up for going out to the bars. "Darling, the sun and sand has drained me." I could tell by the way he averted his eyes he was lying. I suspected he was eager to get back to the B&B. Any draining back there, I supposed, would occur due to the ministrations of our Egyptian host. I couldn't blame Boutros. I had hopes in a similar vein.

"I get it. It's been a long day," I told him, giving no clue that I might be a little suspicious of the "exhausted" routine. It was okay, really. I was looking forward to exploring the bars on my own and had no need for a wingman. In fact, I was thinking that I'd probably have a much greater chance of getting lucky if I was on my own.

And getting lucky was never far from my thoughts.

As I wandered the streets, night fell around me. I'd had it in mind to check out a dance club a German couple I'd run into in the B&B's parlor had told me about. One of them seemed very keen to see me there. And I, of course, wasn't averse to the idea. I was always up for making new friends! And for making a sandwich, if you catch my drift.

Once again, I found myself lost in mazelike streets. Brighton wasn't quite as daunting as London, so I wasn't too worried. I always had the Atlantic as a reference point, and so the wandering took on a more leisurely tone, rather than one of desperation like my first night in London.

And then I saw him. Again.

Across a cobbled, narrow street, he was making his way in the opposite direction. The dim streetlights revealed his longish red-brown hair and the tight fit of his plain white T-shirt, faded Levi's, and Adidas trainers.

I paused to check him out, recalling seeing him stopped in traffic earlier in the day. His body, long and lanky, was even better than the one I'd imagined for him.

I grinned. I'd fully believed we'd never see each other again. That we were simply two ships that passed in the night—or, in this case, a car and pedestrian that passed in the morning. Whatever.

He'd gotten wise to my stare and had slowed to regard me.

Right there in the salt air, the dusky darkness, and the ancient town, our eyes met across the street, and it was just like when he spied me from his car—the earth stood still, and all the normal sights and sounds stopped for just a moment. Have you ever seen the movie *West Side Story*? If you have, you'll probably remember the scene where Tony first sees Maria across the gym dance floor. The world didn't swirl with colors like in the movie, but there was a similar and equally magical connection.

Like we were the only two men in Brighton.

Of course, a moment like that doesn't last forever. A group of college-age guys, half in the bag, passed between us, breaking the electricity of our stares and somehow managing to unmute the world with their raucous laughter and crude insults thrown casually at each other.

We smiled. He made a little gesture to motion me over.

He didn't have to signal twice. I hurried across the cobblestone street to stand before him. The same electric tingle I'd gotten in the past when I'd been up close to a celebrity washed over me. Not that he was a celebrity. Well, he could have been, but what I'm trying to get at was that being near him seemed a little unreal. Larger than life.

"Hi," I said shyly, cursing myself inwardly for not being wittier, more in command of my opening lines. Suddenly shy, I stared down at my sneakers.

I didn't know why. Usually, I was quite bold when on the hunt, but being with this man made me feel I was with a character from one of my favorite books who had magically sprung to life. Abashed, I looked up at him (he had a good two inches on me, and I was already wondering when I could get some of his other inches in me) and noticed how pale brown his eyes were, with the tiniest flecks of yellow in them. And his lashes! Almost too long to be considered masculine, but he was every bit male.

"Hey there," he responded. "How are *you* doing?"

"You're American!" I gasped. "Do you mean to tell me I've come all this way to meet an American? Come on!" I laughed.

He smiled. "Just your rotten luck, huh? Worse, I'm a New Englander, by way of California." He shook his head. "I can't imagine a more hideous hybrid."

I felt bad. "No, no! I didn't mean I was disappointed. I just expected to end up tonight in the arms of an Irishman, or a young Tom Jones lookalike from Wales." *Or a German with a big uncut kielbasa.*

"Who said anything about ending up in my arms?" He took a shocked step back. "Presumptuous. That's what you are."

Heat rushed to my face. There was no way out of this gracefully, so I plowed onward. "Well, did I imagine the look you gave me from across the street?" I snickered a bit, or maybe it was more like a high-pitched and embarrassing titter. I was *so* nervous. "Or from your car?"

Now it was his turn to blush. He pointed at me. "That *was* you! In the street. The most gorgeous man in all of Brighton."

"Well, at least in the top ten, right?" I said weakly.

"No, number one." His smile was kind. "Definitely at the top."

"Or the bottom," I said, with a little Groucho Marx eyebrow wiggle.

We grew silent. I suspect we were both anxious, both feeling a little foolish. And both, I hoped, amazingly turned on.

He jerked a thumb over his shoulder. With a horrible British accent, he asked, "Fancy a pint, mate?"

I noticed for the first time that we were standing in front of a Tudor-looking pub that appeared to be about a thousand years old, all rotting wood and dark stained glass. Now that he mentioned it, the smell of hops and cigarette smoke drifted out, borne on the current of a woman in a red dress exiting the bar, er, pub. I looked up at the swinging sign above our heads. The place was called the Spotted Dick.

"Spotted Dick? That's not something I'm going to catch from you, is it?"

He chuckled. "Not if we use a condom." He shook his head. "No, in these parts, a spotted dick is a custard, a sweet, a pudding, if you will."

"Well," I drew out the word. "I generally avoid dicks that are spotted, but I'll make an exception in your case, since you're so damn cute."

"And American?"

"I'll try not to hold that against you."

"What will you hold against me?"

"Oh Lord, is this going to turn into one of those 'if I told you you had a beautiful body, would you hold it against me' moments? Please say no."

"I'm not that corny. So, do you want to get a beer?"

I stepped away from him and swung open the heavy dark-wood door. Inside, I eyed the crowd, which consisted of a lot of bearded, middle-aged men at the bar with a rowdy group of college-age guys playing darts behind them. I had a feeling this wasn't a gay club. I stepped back out. "Do you think we could have that beer outside? That doesn't really look like our kind of place."

"Our kind of place? Whatever do you mean?"

I rolled my eyes. "Just see if you can get a couple pints to bring outside. That is, if it's not against the law. If they say no, they say no. We can certainly find another place." I groped in my pocket for a few pound notes.

He wagged a finger at me. "Put your money away. It's on me."

"On one condition. As long as it obligates me later, I'm okay with that."

He cocked his head, grinning, and disappeared inside.

While he was gone, I settled on the sidewalk, sitting cross-legged, back against the bar's façade. I figured it must have been getting later, because I noticed the street traffic—both motored and foot-powered—had slowed down. The quiet calmed me (I'd heard the Brits say, "I was in a right state!" and I understood the sentiment). I imagined I could hear the rush of the sea to the shore, although practically, the Atlantic was too far away for that, and I was probably only hearing the ebb and flow of traffic. I rubbed my arms, even though the temperature was probably in the eighties. I'd heard a radio story in passing earlier that day that said the UK was in the midst of a heat wave. A man had died of heatstroke at Blackpool Sands when he'd fallen asleep while sunbathing.

Although I had a pretty good idea, I wondered where tonight would go.

It occurred to me that I didn't even know this guy's name, despite my presentiment that he might turn out to be someone more special than my average trick.

I leaned my head back against the wall and closed my eyes for a second. I had an image of falling through space, almost dreamlike.

Then the door behind me creaked open, and he returned, holding two plastic cups of dark beer.

He settled beside me and handed me mine. "Guinness. I hope you like the stuff. It's supposed to be full of iron."

"To make me strong?"

He bumped his glass against mine. "I bet you're pretty strong anyway. Just look at you. Those guns don't exactly say ninety-eight pound weakling." He smiled, and I got a jolt when he ran a hand over one of my biceps. "No, if anything maybe the iron will give you a little added endurance." He very skillfully raised one eyebrow, and his grin was of the cat-that-ate-the-canary variety.

"For what?" I asked, all innocence.

"Oh, I can't imagine."

"I bet you can." I wanted to smile, but suddenly, the sexual tension in the heated air amped up to a boil. I couldn't find words, so I simply stared at him, knowing how hungry I looked.

He regarded me with the same naked hunger and then took a sip of his Guinness. His cheeks puffed out with the dark liquid. He crooked his finger at me to come forward. I did, and he pressed his mouth to mine, transferring the ale from his mouth to mine. Normally, I would have had a *yuck* moment, but this was incredibly sexy, so intimate that I immediately got rock hard.

I swallowed and raised my hand to the back of his neck to draw him closer. Hungrily, I probed the inside of his mouth with my tongue. Again that sensation of falling away, replaced with his presence, simply filled up my world.

When we pulled apart, I was winded and a little shaky. Let's face it—at that point in my life, I was, to put it baldly, a slut. Jaded. I loved men. I loved their bodies, their cocks, their asses, their chests, the way their thighs looked spread wide, their smiles, their eyes, and how they smelled, especially if they *hadn't* recently showered. So, the fact that I was on the verge of trembling and all but breathless really said something.

My libido had gone to such a hot place, I was like those cartoon thermometers you may have seen where the mercury explodes out of the top. Except it wasn't mercury exploding out of the top I saw in my mind's eye.

"Are you okay?" he whispered in my ear and gave a small, exquisitely painful bite to the lobe.

I twisted with discomfort because the front of my shorts was so tight. "No. No, sir, I am not."

"Do we need to get you somewhere where you can be seen? Where someone can perhaps make you all better?" Again that low whisper in my ear, almost a growl. It was making the hair on my neck stand up. It was making me leak farther south. I shifted again and laughed, swatting at him.

"Like a hospital?" I gulped.

"No, silly. Do you have a place?"

I stared at him, ready to tear his clothes off right here on the street. Ready to tear *my own* clothes off right here on the street, roll on my back, and toss my legs in the air, crying, "Come on, big boy, fill me up!" I could just about do it, too, blind as I was with red-hazed and lustful hunger.

But I did have a shred—just a shred, mind you—of propriety and common sense. These were two qualities I had yet to master drawing heavily upon, so that shred was mighty strained. I gasped, "But I don't even know your name."

He sat up a little straighter. "You wouldn't believe me if I told you."

That cooled the fires raging inside me a little. Was he, perhaps, a boy named Sue? Was he something embarrassing? Wilbur, maybe? God forbid—Marion?

Was he an infamous killer on the lam? Was there an international search in progress for him at this very moment?

Would he turn out to be my long-lost brother? The product of my mother's secret teenage pregnancy and her giving the baby up for adoption? Was there an intuitive part of me yanking me away from the horror of incest?

I had to laugh at myself. Someday, I'd have to write this shit down. I said, "Seriously. If we're going anywhere for treatment, I would need a name. First and last, preferably. And don't bullshit me."

"Well, what's yours?"

"Ricky. Ricky Comparetto."

"Ah, an Italian."

"Sicilian, to be precise. On my mom's side. You're stalling."

He took in a deep breath, smiled a little nervously and a lot charmingly, and came out with it. "Walt. Walt Whitman."

"No!"

"Yes. 'Happiness not in another place, but this place, not for another hour, but this hour.'" His brown eyes were soulful.

"Whitman?" I asked.

"Of course. You get awfully familiar when you're someone's namesake." He extended a hand.

I looked at it quizzically for a moment and then caught on. I shook it. "Pleased to meet you, Walt."

"Ricky. Charmed."

He said my name with such warmth that I was, paradoxically, chilled. "I love that quote, though." My mind lingered over the words, especially the part about happiness being this hour. "Are we going to find happiness...right here? Right now?"

"I hope so. But perhaps not exactly *right* here. I don't cotton to going to jail tonight for public indecency. And believe me, boy, the things I have in mind for you are not only indecent but bordering on perverse."

"Only bordering?" I asked, disappointed. "You don't have a place?" I considered bringing him to the room I shared with Boutros, but there was the serious risk he could already be there, alone or with the Egyptian or God-knew-who-else. Or, even worse, he could barge in at a very inopportune moment, and I would be forced to wave at him with my toes atop Walt's broad shoulders.

Walt shook his head. "I'm staying at someone's house, just outside of town. I'm part of this travel network where we share our places when we travel. It's cheap. But not always private." He sighed. "For one, it's about an hour's drive. And two, it's truly against my host's rules to bring home a guest, even one as charming as yourself."

"I get it. He doesn't want come stains on the chintz."

"Something like that. So you're saying you don't have a place either?" He looked thoughtful for a moment. "There are the bushes opposite the beach. But we wouldn't be alone, and as much as I might occasionally enjoy putting on a show, that's not what I want for us tonight—not for our first time." He put a finger to his chin. "There's always my car, but it's cramped, and I don't know how acrobatic I'm feeling. Again, there's the whole public thing—even in a car with steamed-up windows—so that's out."

I was quiet for a while. I reasoned with myself that Boutros was my best friend. He'd understand if I brought someone home, wouldn't he? He'd be happy to hang out in the lounge or wherever for at least a little while. It was the kind of thing best friends did for each other—especially where men were concerned.

I moaned inwardly, disappointed that I hadn't already had a good discussion with him about this very thing. We could have at least worked out a signal—a sock tied to the doorknob, maybe.

My desire, not surprisingly, won out over any caution. Boutros would have to understand, and if he didn't, fuck him. I had me a man!

A man that I suspected, against all logic, might be more than a one-trick pony. So I said, "I have a room in the B&B a couple streets over."

Walt leaned in, eager, listening. "And we can walk there?"

I nodded. "But listen, I have a roommate. He may or may not already be there, asleep. In which case we will be sorely out of luck." I kissed Walt quickly. "And we may have to simply make use of that car or those bushes. Because, honey, there's no way I'm going to part ways with you tonight without feeling you inside me." *Wow. That was bold enough, right?*

I went on. "My buddy and I share our bed. There's just the one."

Walt eyed me. He asked, quite reasonably, "Are you sure he's only a buddy?"

"Positive. I'm blissfully single." I looked into his eyes. "For now."

We'd made a decision. I cemented it further by standing and reaching out with my hand to help Walt up.

When we were both standing and ready to head off, I added, "If he's there and asleep, we will find a way."

Walt nodded. "Where there's a will..."

"Or in this case, where there's a Walt..."

"You're hopeless."

We set off into the darkness.

*

The B&B was alive with light and laughter. In the common room, what the Egyptian and his British lover called the lounge, there was a large group gathered, most of whom, I was sure, weren't staying there.

I peered into the room from the front door, Walt looking over my shoulder. A cloud of smoke rolled toward us, like a blue-gray fog, a potent mixture of tobacco and cannabis.

Someone was playing an accordion fitfully. I heard a snatch of that old Big Band standard, "Mairzy Doats," which stopped as suddenly as it began. There was weak applause and much laughter. Then the accordionist started in on "Days of Wine and Roses." Lord!

Mostly men occupied the room, of all shapes, sizes, ages, and races. But there were a few women too—an exotic looking Asian woman sat off by herself in a corner, wrapped in a large blue satin pashmina, smoking a pipe. Hashish? I wondered. Next to her a voluptuous redhead, her hair a mass of tight-knit curls, her eyes big and brown, was reading, seemingly undisturbed by the raucous laughter and loud conversation. The book open on her lap was Henry Miller's *Tropic of Capricorn*. Something she read caused her to throw back her head and emit an earsplitting shriek of laughter. At least I think it was laughter.

Had no one here ever heard of "inside voices"?

And I clutched and squeezed Walt's hand, still in mine, the sweat from both gluing us together, when I saw, with great relief, Boutros come in from the kitchen. He had a pint of beer in one hand and a cigarette in the other. The Egyptian was close by, following like a dark shadow— or a puppy. Boutros was ignoring him but pointedly so.

I smiled and turned to Walt. "We're in the clear. Let's get upstairs while the room is still empty. I don't know how long it'll stay that way."

We were up the stairs practically without our feet touching the treads.

I unlocked the door, let Walt precede me, then followed him in. I shut the door behind me, smiling and a little breathless. The door was heavy and the sounds of the party downstairs were almost completely obliterated.

I eyed Walt and burst into laughter. Not because this was funny—although it did have its humorous side—but because, after so much worry that this could not possibly happen tonight, it finally was.

He pressed against me, flattening me against the door with his body. A surge like electricity—blue and white— coursed through me. I visualized sparks. My dick, never less than half-mast, flared into full-on iron bar erection. In books, they're always talking about someone's heart skipping a beat, and I don't think mine did, but it sure as hell sped up. So did my pulse. Beads of sweat broke out simultaneously on my forehead and at the base of my spine. The slow crawl of one down my back tickled.

Our mouths locked together. Our crotches ground. Someone was moaning, and I wasn't sure if it was me, Walt, or both of us. I went weak in the knees. Was an onset of the vapors far behind?

We continued this behavior for several more minutes, stoking the fire so much I was certain that with one more movement on Walt's part, no matter how simple, I would explode, filling my pants with premature DNA.

Out of self-preservation, I pushed him roughly away.

He stumbled back and regarded me, panting. His lips looked bruised. His face was red, both from desire and the sandpaper of my several-day-old beard. His eyes, I swear, were alive with light, flashing. He looked like a bull, ready to charge. My fuck-or-flee instinct was aroused.

I breathed heavily for a moment, getting that heart rate and pulse more in check, waiting for the spasms in my dick to die down. I was nearly at the point of spurting like a volcano.

"Just wait," I begged. "Give me one minute. Just. One. Minute."

"Okay, but that's it. One."

I watched him move back toward the bed. He plopped down on it, pulled off his shoes, and flung them into opposite corners. He yanked down his pants and boxers all at once. His uncut dick sprang up, proud, and slapped against his flat belly. In a flash, he pulled his shirt gracefully over his head.

He sat naked before me, legs spread, eyes pleading, dick twitching—a Colt fantasy come to life.

It was the most beautiful sight I'd ever seen. And that's saying a lot, because I was no stranger to seeing many, many men similarly presented.

I wanted him with a passion that went beyond words, exceeded reason, existed on a plane far above mere lust.

I felt dizzy.

But not dizzy enough to repress my pounce instinct.

I shed my clothes in a blur and came to him. Our lips joined together once more, while our hands, like independent beasts, began roaming over the other's body, pausing to tweak, fondle, caress.

Our movements in the brightly lit room could have been choreographed. The touching, grasping, kissing, and sucking went on for what seemed, paradoxically, like a very short time and for what seemed like forever. At least I didn't want it to ever stop! But there was a sense that we'd always been in this moment. Surreal and hyperreal, all at the same time.

And then Walt had me at the edge of the bed. He stood between my legs, his dick rising up between them. My own dick twitched above my belly. A line of precome pooled in my navel.

Walt reached down to grab a drop of it with his fingertip and then put it to his lips. "Sweet." He swallowed. "Now please tell me you have condoms."

I smiled. "And lube. In the nightstand drawer. Hurry."

He found the supplies we'd need, donned the condom quickly, and positioned himself between my legs. He looked down at me and frowned. Not the reaction I was hoping for.

"What? What's wrong? Just put it in me, please!" I pulled him forward by his thighs with my feet. He put a hand on my stomach to stop me.

He then took in a deep breath, teased my hole with the sheathed head of his cock. He pulled back, stroking himself. "I need to tell you something."

"What? Can't it wait?"

He shook his head, and sadness flickered across those fine features.

"What?" I asked. "Nothing you can say is going to stop that dick from going deep inside."

"Are you sure?" He cocked his head. "How about the fact that I'm—"

I interrupted, knowing where this was going. It was the midnineties, and I was a very sexually active gay man. I knew what he was about to say, so I finished for him. "You're HIV-positive."

"Is that okay?"

"In the big scheme of things? No, I wish you didn't have that virus in your system. But it doesn't change what I want, where I want it, and when I want it, which is *now*, dammit. You've got a rubber on, for Christ's sake. The CDC says that's a pretty good barrier. So, shove it in! And, for the love of God, please *don't* be gentle."

He grinned at me and shook his head. He needed no further encouragement. He slid the length of himself inside me with one mighty thrust, and there was no pain, only the most intense pleasure that made me cry out in what I recognized as an exhilarated scream.

The fucking was raw and intense, brutal. The headboard knocked against the wall so hard, I expected to see plaster dust in the air. The bed frame shook. The box springs squeaked. Both of us made a lot of noise until we realized—or rather, it was brought to our attention—that the window was wide open and the lights were on.

We'd also failed to draw either the draperies or the blinds.

When we heard the first voice from outside, we moved off the bed. I was on the floor on my hands and knees, with Walt behind me, when I heard a shout from the building across the way. "Keep it down, fellas. Some of us are trying to sleep."

Walt kept pounding, his balls slapping against my ass.

A second later, there was a wolf whistle and applause floating up from the street below. A different voice shouted, "And some of us are enjoying the show. Bravo, fellas."

I didn't care. Walt didn't care. He thrust faster and faster into me, and swear to God, I could feel the powerful spasms as he unloaded inside me, groaning. He gripped my hips so hard I thought the imprint of his fingers would be there for days. I looked down to see a puddle of come below my belly and my dick attached to it by a long strand of come. Is it good or bad when you're so in the moment you don't even realize you're coming until you see the physical evidence?

Let's call it good.

It was at that precise moment that Boutros burst into the room, the Egyptian in hot pursuit.

"Jesus Christ," I heard one of them mumble.

"Playing leapfrog...again?" That time I knew who was speaking—Boutros—always with the quips!

I glanced over my shoulder, and over Walt, still in position behind me. I was heaving, not sure I'd ever be able to breathe again. The facility of my imagination, though, continued to work, and I saw myself and my latest paramour through Boutros's eyes.

And I couldn't help it. Despite my shortness of breath, I began to laugh, chuckling at first, and finally guffawing so hard, I collapsed to the carpet below me, rolling around in my own sticky-wet.

Walt became disengaged, naturally, and he joined me in my laughter, his head bouncing on my ass.

From the floor, I peered again at Boutros, staring slack-jawed at us with the Egyptian leering over his shoulder and actually licking his lips.

"Oh!" Boutros cried. "This is too delicious for words."

"Shall we join them?" the Egyptian asked, eager.

Boutros appeared startled, as though he'd forgotten one of our hosts stood directly behind him. He turned for a moment and then gave him a little push. "Leave me alone, Anwar! I think I hear your husband calling."

Anwar's dark eyes widened, and he scurried away.

"Is it all right if I come in, then? I'm not going to get anything on me, am I?" Without waiting for an answer, Boutros slipped inside. He shut the door behind him.

I got up. Stooped to pick up my T-shirt from the floor and used it to wipe away the come on my chest and belly and to clear the lube out from the crack of my ass. I perched on the side of the bed.

Walt, visibly shaken, moved to stand near the draperies, almost hidden behind them. He reminded me of Boo Radley at the end of *To Kill a Mockingbird*. I think he was trying to make himself invisible.

Boutros sauntered over to the other side of the bed. He sat opposite me and leaned over to light a cigarette. Holding it between his teeth, he looked over his shoulder to examine the sheets.

"Is it okay?" I asked. "Do you feel safe to lie down?" I was gradually getting my breath back. My heart rate and pulse were slowly but surely returning to normal. The world was coming back into focus. I wondered what to do about Walt.

"Well, there's no *obvious* evidence on the sheets of recent anal penetration."

"No skid marks or blood?"

"Precisely," Boutros said. "So I guess I can sleep here tonight."

He looked over at Walt, cowering in the corner. "Where's he going to sleep?"

Walt, red-faced and trembling a bit, moved out of the corner to begin gathering up his clothes and getting himself dressed. I had to admit, I felt a little sorry for him.

Walt spoke to Boutros, "I'm going. I'm going. Sorry!"

Boutros lay back on the bed and stared up at the ceiling, toward which he blew a massive cloud of smoke. "Now darling, don't get yourself into a snit. You're welcome to stay, but I'm afraid either you or Ricky will have to sleep on the floor. I'm not giving up my side of the bed. I'm exhausted." He rolled over on his side and then extended a hand. "Boutros BinBin. So pleased to make your acquaintance."

Walt stared down at the hand. "Is that your real name?"

Oh, that's rich, I thought.

"It's as real as I say it is, sweetheart."

They shook hands, and Walt appeared to relax a little. He was dressed now. I couldn't believe that it had been only a few minutes ago that he'd been naked, sweating, and inside me.

"Who are you?" Boutros asked. He glanced at me. "Or haven't you gotten around to exchanging more than bodily fluids yet?"

I rolled my eyes. "His name is Walt. Walt Whitman."

Boutros took a drag. "Sure it is."

"I really should be going," Walt said, a sickly smile affixed to those oh-so-handsome features.

"I'll walk you out." I started toward the door.

"Like that?" Boutros asked.

It was then I realized I hadn't bothered to put any clothes on. I sighed, stooped down to snatch my blue plaid boxers off the floor, and struggled into them. I didn't think anyone below would have a problem with my attire, even without the boxers.

Once we'd made it through the revelers in the lounge, by now down to a dedicated half dozen, Walt and I stood outside in the relatively cool night air on the front stoop.

"Tonight was more than just hot," I told Walt. "If it doesn't sound too corny, it was kind of magical."

He gave me a quick kiss and said softly, "It doesn't sound corny. And I agree."

We stood together like that for a while, enjoying the wan illumination cast by a crescent moon and the briny breeze rising up now and again. We both, I suspected, needed some cooling off.

"I hope you don't have to go too far to get to where you're staying."

"This time of night, it won't be bad."

"I can walk you to your car." Suddenly, I didn't want to let go of the tenuous connection we'd forged.

"You don't need to. I'm looking forward to the walk, when Brighton is still for a change. Really, I'm okay. I need the walk to allow that werewolf I became to fully get back inside."

"I liked that werewolf being fully inside. Oh yes, I did. Very much. Please sir, can I have some more?"

He smiled. Ran his fingers across my cheek. He nodded. "Am I ever gonna see you again?"

"I certainly hope so." I stared into his eyes. "We're here through tomorrow. Then, we're heading to Boutros's hometown."

"Which is where? Never Never Land? The Island of Misfit Toys?"

I laughed. "Something like that." I drew in the night air, exhaled slowly. "Bath."

"Ah, the home of Cheap Street and Gay Street. You'll love it. But stay out of the baths. They're toxic."

And with those parting words, he leaned in to kiss me very briefly, yet very sweetly. Then he turned and disappeared into the night.

I was pretty sure I'd never see him again. A bittersweet thought.

I was wrong.

Chapter Seven

The sound of our door creaking open woke me. Through half-closed eyes, I watched Boutros tiptoe into the room. Brilliant sunlight illuminated him in a thin slat through the opening between the window curtains. And even in that restricted light, I could read the mixture of shame and satisfaction on his face.

I groaned and turned over. The Westclox Bakelite alarm on the nightstand told me it was only a little after six.

Boutros froze in his tracks as though he were a cat burglar who'd just slipped in through an open window and spied a growling pit bull.

I got up on my elbows. "Where've you been? Isn't it awfully early to be out and about?"

He grinned at me and raised his eyebrows. "Apparently, it's not for some of us. The cock has crowed!"

"You went to those bushes across from the nude beach, didn't you?" I would have been jealous, but my ass was still smarting from last night. *Give it a rest, Mary!* Ah, sweet tactile memories of love.

"Yes. It was wonderful. I bumped into a lovely young thing from Leeds. I caught him spitting out a mouthful of jizz just as the sun was rising. Very romantic! I asked him, 'What the hell was that?' and do you know what he said?"

I settled back on the pillow. "No."

"He said, 'My last love affair.' And then this sweet boy raised his eyebrows at me in a most fetching manner. 'Do you fancy being my next?'"

"I bet he didn't have to ask you twice."

"No, sir, he did not." Boutros giggled. Giggling was rare for him. "But I did come twice," he said in a whisper.

"Wonderful. Now, some of us need to get a little more sleep."

Boutros tore off the athletic shorts and tank top he wore and crawled into bed. He cuddled up next to me. I rolled away.

The last thing I recall before drifting off was him reminding me that we were off to Bath today. "Home of the ancient Roman baths," he told me. "And buns with clotted cream."

Now the latter sounded quite interesting...

*

We arrived at Bath Spa station late in the afternoon, among a whole crowd of jovial summer travelers. There was a sense of excitement in the music of their murmurs, the heat of the late-afternoon sun, and the sheer history of the city we'd just arrived in.

"Just the other side of the station is the River Avon," Boutros said, and it made me immediately think of William Shakespeare (as in Stratford-upon-Avon). Little did I know that the parking lot for the Bath Spa station, right along the river's banks, would very soon have a much more erotic association. "But we're not going that way." Boutros maneuvered us through the crowds and led me outside.

Across the street from the station were a lot of charming little shops, restaurants, and cafés. The town appeared to consist of a mix of mostly old and ornate buildings, rising up three stories or so, and more modern ones that, I admitted to myself, looked ugly next to their elder, statelier sisters. In the distance, tree-covered hills rose up.

"It's just full of charm, isn't it?" Boutros paused for a moment beside me to look around. He lit a cigarette.

"You're being sarcastic?" I never knew with him, even though we'd been best friends for going on five years now.

"No, silly. I grew up here, so I tend to take it for granted. But now, seeing it through your eyes...well, it's really quite lovely." He scanned the horizon.

Bath certainly wasn't lacking in either charm or history. I felt a little rush of warmth and affection for Boutros, who so rarely displayed a softer side. I still couldn't help but expect he'd cut in with some cruel remark. He'd warned me on the train how crazy his family was, his mother in particular. "That bitch is psychic. Just a fun fact. She also delights in making my life miserable. You'll see."

"Did you mean psychotic?" I asked.

"That too." He also mentioned his ex-wife, who still lived here with three children Boutros had fathered back in the day. "When I was drunk," he explained. "You'll find Beryl holding up the bar, hoping to cadge as many free drinks as she can. She was pretty once, but now? Face like a smacked ass."

Ah, there he was—the Boutros I knew and loved!

"Are you hungry? Or would you rather just get to our hosts'?"

We would be staying with a young gay couple who lived off one of the many crescents in the city, up the hill from the station. Boutros said we wouldn't require a cab.

The couple, Philip and Teddy, had lived together for only a short time, but, Boutros warned me, Teddy, the product of what he called a "public school" education, had a wandering eye. "So, don't go causing any trouble, you home-wrecker!"

"I only have eyes for Walt." I winked. "Walt Whitman."

"If you believe that's his real name—" Boutros began.

I finished for him, "Then I must believe Boutros BinBin is yours."

We headed up and up and up the narrow streets until we came, out of breath, to a relatively modern apartment building—white brick with black shutters and a black-and-white awning over the front door.

"Remember what I told you," Boutros whispered as we approached. "Teddy is off-limits. They're nice enough to let us stay with them. We don't need you spreading your gonorrhea around to my friends."

"Shut up."

Boutros rang their buzzer.

"Besides," I went on. "I got that cleared up before we came over."

Boutros rolled his eyes. "I'm sure only to make room for yet another venereal disease, if I know you!"

"You are so mean." I thought for a second. "Teddy is off-limits, or so you say, but what about Philip?"

"I thought you only had eyes for Mr. Whitman. Shame on you. Besides, Philip is, from what Teddy's told me, unfailingly monogamous."

"How bourgeois. How boring."

A startling buzz interrupted, letting us know we could go inside.

The boys, as I soon began calling them, were charming. They'd laid out a proper tea for us, and I was impressed, although I did make the faux pas of referring to it as high tea.

Teddy corrected me. "It's actually afternoon tea. High tea, despite sounding pinkie-in-the-air lofty, is actually a working-class convention." Teddy smiled, and despite my fondness for Mr. Whitman, I was already charmed by his wavy chestnut hair and gray eyes. The way he stared so deeply into *my* eyes told me he might have been more than a little charmed by me as well. I could see we'd be navigating some dangerous territory during this visit.

His boyfriend, Philip, broke our ocular connection by setting a cup and saucer before me. He started with me but then put out cups for everyone on their small walnut dining table.

Philip was what I suppose people refer to as "Black Irish." He had dark curly hair, and where Teddy was lithe and taut-muscled, Philip was a beefy man with a bit of gut. His smile was warm as he held the matching teapot aloft and asked, "Shall I be mother?"

I giggled nervously. "I don't know what that means," I said. I'd heard the expression before, but had forgotten to ask what it meant. I expected him to disappear, perhaps, into the adjacent bedroom and reemerge as Norman Bates's mom. Or the Queen Mum in a gray wig, sensible frock, and crown.

Boutros looked at me like the heathen I'm sure they all thought I was. "It just means he'll pour."

Teddy leaned close. "And give you a little sugar, if you're good. And he's always happy to give you some cream, if you're so inclined."

I stared at him for a moment, wondering if this was simply regular *afternoon* tea talk or some serious double entendre.

Boutros spoke for me once the tea, a lovely Darjeeling, had been poured. "Give him lots of cream and sugar. Me too."

Teddy eyed me. "Like your tea like you like your men, then?"

"How's that?" I pushed my cup forward so Philip could add cream and a couple of sugar cubes.

"Sweet and white."

"Um, I keep an open mind about men...and tea." Heat rose in my cheeks. Teddy was making me already feel oddly aroused and a little nauseous. I sipped the too-hot tea and surveyed the food they'd laid out for us. I leaned forward and pointed. "So, tell me what we have here."

Philip obliged. "Egg salad," he began, pointing to the sandwiches, which were cut into quarters with the crusts thoughtfully removed. "Vanilla scones. Cheese and pickle. Lemon tart." Philip eyed Teddy with what I believed was fondness. "Teddy made the lemon curd himself."

"My curd is delicious," Teddy said.

"I'll bet." I eyed him.

We moved on to other topics of conversation, and I was glad. I was feeling decidedly unsafe around the predatory—and quite sexy—Teddy. We talked about the heat wave and what we'd do that evening.

*

Bath had only one gay bar, the Snooty Pig, and even that was only half a bar. Let me explain—the bar was divided into two main rooms. One entered through a common entrance and then decided which way to go. If you were of the gay persuasion—or, as Teddy said, preferred sausage over pie—you veered off to the left. If you only had eyes for the opposite sex, you headed right.

Each room was essentially the same, dominated by a long oak bar, behind which were mirrors and rows and rows of spirits. There were taps for cider, ales, and lagers. A padded bench ran in an L-shape along the back wall of each room, and that was about it for seating. Neither bar had bar stools. At the end of the bar was a wire display that held crisps in interesting varieties—like ketchup or marmite or even steak-flavored.

"I'd steer well clear of those if I were you." Boutros eyed me. He patted my belly. "We don't want this getting any bigger, now, do we?"

I frowned. "I'll have you know I am only nine percent body fat." I patted my flat stomach, making sure it was still there.

"And nine percent moral as well."

I shrugged. "Depends on your definition of morality." My morality included a particular type of kindness to strangers, usually administered lovingly while on my knees, on all fours, or on my back with my knees resting near my ears. This was a sweet kind of compassion—one enjoyed by both the giver and receiver (and those roles could shift delightfully back and forth).

"The restroom downstairs is common," Boutros whispered in my ear.

"What do you care how it's decorated?"

We picked up our beer from the bartender, Boutros reminding me once again not to tip, and moved to the back, where Teddy and Philip were already seated.

Boutros sat, while I hovered near him. In a gay bar, my main goal was always to remain clearly visible to anyone who might be scanning the crowd. "I wasn't talking about the décor, you half-wit." He took a sip.

"Well, what do you mean, then, when you say the restroom is common?"

Teddy overheard. "He means that the men's loo is for both sides of the bar." He grinned. "So mind whose purple parsnip you're checking out!"

The boys collapsed into laughter. Once I caught onto what a purple parsnip was, I joined in.

Philip added, "Late at night, the blokes from the straight side of the bar—" He made air quotes around the word straight. "—can be more open-minded, if you know what I mean."

Teddy said, "The later the hour, the more alcohol consumed, the more willing the man."

I nodded. "Gotcha." Setting down my beer, I said, "I think I'll go take a piss."

The men's room was a disappointment. Perhaps it was too early, but I was the only one in the subway-tiled room with its long trough and two stalls. I lingered for a while, staring into the big mirror over the sink, fussing with my hair, hoping someone interesting and interested might pop in. I was not above adjourning to the stall with a "bloke" if he was cute enough, never mind that I'd "fallen in love" only the night before. And once in the relative privacy of that stall, I thought, smiling to myself, all bets were off on what was out of bounds.

After what seemed like an hour, but was really only a hopeful five minutes, I gave up, vowing to return later on when my bladder was full and my holes were more in need of filling and drilling.

I felt lucky.

When I returned to the bar, I saw my three friends engaged in deep conversation, their heads angled near one another's. Boutros was rolling his eyes, Teddy was laughing, and Philip was morosely shaking his head. Not wanting to interrupt, and suddenly feeling the urge to be alone for a few minutes, I cut through the crowd in the bar and stepped outside. I hadn't been alone since we left Brighton earlier that day, and I was really feeling the need for some me time.

In case you might not have guessed (and how could you with the behavior I've thus far recounted?), I'm a total introvert. A quiet lad. Shy, despite my shameless tendencies where good-looking men were concerned. Despite the ability to be outgoing (Boutros would say slutty), I truly needed alone time to recharge and refuel. If I didn't get it, I could get...cranky. I was now approaching that point—it had come upon me suddenly and without warning.

Once outside, being by myself caused me to release a big, relieved exhale. I took in my surroundings once more. The sky was a lovely color—if I were to recreate it from a crayon box, I'd choose cornflower blue and lavender as my main choices, with a dash of orange near the horizon. Up high, a few stars twinkled. The street in front of the Snooty Pig was blessedly quiet, as most of the town's revelers had already headed inside, choosing gay or straight or a mix of the two down below in the restrooms.

I found a bench a little way from the entrance and gratefully sat, stretched out my legs, and closed my eyes for a moment, breathing in the dusky night air. I wondered what the sleeping arrangements would be at Teddy and Philip's, wondered further if I could keep my hands off Teddy, especially if he encouraged me. Resisting the advances of a good-looking man was as foreign to me, as...well...the country I was now visiting.

Not to be vain, but I truly wondered if Teddy could keep his hands off me. I'd seen the way he eyed me the moment we met. I knew the look because I had handed it out quite often myself.

Would Boutros resent my sleeping with one of his homeland friends? As much as I pretended not to care, I did.

I opened my eyes when I sensed, beneath my eyelids, someone standing near. I expected to see Boutros. He'd be coming out to urge me to get back inside and be more social.

But it wasn't Boutros.

No, it was a face I hadn't expected and certainly hadn't dared hope I would see again.

I smiled. "Walt." I drew out his name, savoring it.

He sat next to me. "I was hoping I'd find you here." He scooted closer so that our shoulders touched.

"This is a wonderful surprise," I confessed with genuine emotion. Most of my encounters with men to date had been of the "once-only" variety, and it was beginning to get on my nerves. What was wrong with me, anyway? I was cute, reasonably smart, and relatively low-maintenance. And now, here was a man I'd fantasized about seeing again but, as with most fantasies, hadn't really dared hope it would come true.

My thoughts of a dalliance with Teddy suddenly went up like a wisp of smoke on the night air. "I wasn't sure you were headed this way."

Walt stretched his long legs out before him and leaned back with a contented sigh. He wore a pair of old jeans, ripped at the knee, and a faded gray T-shirt with an image of Salvador Dali on the front. He'd pulled his long chestnut hair back into a ponytail. "I wasn't sure I was either. That's the beauty of this trip—to just go off wherever, with no agenda." He glanced over at me and smiled. "I love to travel."

"Oh, I do too. I just wish I could afford to do more of it." I thought of my cubicle back in Chicago, where the work would be piling up. I'd pay dearly in time for this trip abroad when I got back. And I didn't even want to think about how I'd pay once the credit card statements rolled in. Boutros kept reminding me that, as much as I thought it so, a pound was really not equal to a dollar.

"You can. You just have to want it. And then you make it happen. It might not always be luxury accommodations. You need to be ready to fly out at a moment's notice when there's a great last-minute deal. Have a bag packed and ready to go. Or, like me, you can hit up travel magazines for assignments if you have a way with words. That's how I pay for a lot of my trips—some magazine sends me out to do a piece. The pay for the work itself is often shit, but the trip is all-expenses paid."

"I never considered doing that. I do have a bit of a flair for writing, if I do say so myself." I thought of the unfinished horror novel on my hard drive at home and the several porno stories I'd had published in magazines like *Stallion* and *Drummer*.

"They're always looking for good writers. It helps if you can take halfway decent pictures too."

He looked over at me and held me in his gaze. "What are we talking about?"

"Travel. I envy you."

"Don't envy me. Or maybe do. I have nothing, really. Most of my stuff can be packed into a single suitcase. I live in a rented room in Boston. But having next to nothing can be very freeing. Most folks, in their quest for material things like houses and cars, don't get that. And they then become slaves to the very things they seek."

I nodded and realized there was more to Walt than a pretty face and a big dick. He had substance and was a thoughtful man, maybe a little unusual. He'd mentioned baggage, of the literal variety, but I suspected he didn't carry much of any kind. I found myself liking him more and more. I wanted to know him better.

"So, is that what brought you here? An assignment?"

He shook his head. "No. This one's all on me. Just for fun. I was enjoying all the scenery, the history. I've already been to Wales, and I hope to get up to Scotland before I have to go back in a couple weeks. As you know, I'm renting a junker car, but it runs, and as long as I can remember to stay on the left side of the road, I should be okay." He grinned.

I wasn't sure what to say. I'd never been so carefree, not like Walt. I didn't know if I could travel the way he did, which seemed to be letting the wind blow him in whatever direction it was going.

"This trip's been great, but I have to confess—it's been a little lonely."

"Yes?" I found that hard to believe. A guy who looked like Walt and had his ease and self-assurance would seem, at least to me, to have no problem finding lots of companionship.

"Yeah." He pushed my hair back off my forehead. "That's why I was so happy when I met you. There's something about you that's different from most of the guys I meet. Believe it or not, I see you as a bit of an old soul. I think there are more layers to you than even you're aware of." He laughed, seeming a little sheepish. "I'm having a bit of trouble getting you out of my head."

Heat surged throughout my whole body. Then my suspicion/low self-esteem kicked in. I turned to give him a wry smile. "Ah, I bet you say that to all the boys."

"Do *not*! Even though I was easy on our first date, if you can even call it a date, I'm not always quick to jump into bed with just anyone. Sure, I get my chances, but I need to feel something more than just animal magnetism—although, honey, I felt plenty of that with you. But there needs to be some of that magic, you know? Something that's hard to put your finger on, but you know it when you feel it. When you look into a person's eyes..."

A lot of glib responses came to mind, but for once I didn't allow myself to utter any of them—I didn't want to. I was touched, genuinely touched, and suppressed the tear or two wanting to well up in my eyes. "I do know what you mean." I suddenly wanted to be with no one else. And, believe me, that went against all imaginings and intentions I'd had before I boarded the plane at O'Hare International. Back in Chicago, my hope was to sample as many "bangers" as possible once I was across the pond.

I was surprising myself. Or maybe not. Maybe what I'd been longing for was sitting right next to me, on a bench in Bath, Somerset, England. And maybe it was no accident that the first man I'd met and really liked on this trip turned out to also be an American. Boston sure wasn't all that close to Chicago, but at least it was on the same continent.

I couldn't help it. I needed to know, so I blurted out, "Did you follow me here?"

He chuckled. "Well, since I was driving and you came via train, no, not literally. But I did come to Bath hoping to run into you again."

I didn't want to let on how happy this made me. I was beaming inside but gave Walt only the glimmer of a smile. "I was hoping to run into you again too."

Walt was leaning forward—to kiss me, I was pretty sure—when two women emerged from the bar.

They were in their twenties, one a brassy platinum blonde with voluptuous curves, hugged lasciviously by the tight, cropped T-shirt and mini skirt she wore. And the other was an even younger woman than the first. I cast her in the role of wingwoman. She was a little on the dowdy side, with very dark straight hair, glasses, and wearing a pair of shorts, a blouse, and flat sandals. Her friend wore towering red heels. The women were chattering and smoking. The language they spoke I barely recognized, despite being certain it was English. Words like "banging," "slapper," and "creps" came out frequently. So did a reference to "fags," but I don't think they were being homophobic.

Walt leaned away from me and stared straight ahead. He dropped his hands between his knees and blew out a big sigh.

"Frustrated?" I asked.

"As hell," he said.

"Want to get out of here?"

"Got a place to go?"

And once more, we were confronted with the same dilemma we'd had in Brighton. I was simply not a "my place" kind of guy, at least over here. "Again," I responded, "I'm not alone. I don't think either of us wants a repeat of what happened in Brighton. Well, I do, some of it at least, but not being caught with our pants down, as it were."

"Do you ever get a room of your own?" Walt laughed.

"Not on this trip. Not on my budget."

Walt leaned close and whispered, "Could I coax you into my car, then?"

"Do you have a candy bar?"

Walt nodded eagerly. "It's six inches long and has two nuts."

"I think you're underestimating yourself. Sounds like an Almond Joy to me."

"Oh, I think it might bring you some joy."

"Some?" I asked.

Walt raised an eyebrow. "A lot."

I stood, and the girls peered over at me. The blonde batted her eyelashes and said, "Brilliant night, innit?"

I looked over at Walt for a translation. He shrugged.

"Either of you lads got a fag you can spare?"

I couldn't resist. I took Walt's arm. "Yeah, I've got one right here. But I can't spare him, sweetheart, so bugger off." I did know some Brit slang, after all.

The good-natured laughter of both women followed us as we left them.

"How far is your car?"

"Just a block or two over."

*

We ended up driving only a very short distance—down to the parking lot by the Bath Spa train station. The lot was nearly empty this time of night, and Walt parked at the edge. The River Avon spread out before us, a magical flow of shimmering black.

We silently took in our river view. I noticed how the moon reflected on its current like a silver wafer out of which someone had taken a bite. It was serene, and there was, for once, blessedly, a bit of chill in the air. A slight odor of fish rose up from the dark waters. In addition to anticipation and lust, a sense of contentment also crept in, a feeling of being at home.

The passage of a small boat, its lights on low, cut through the night.

"Beautiful," I said.

Walt turned to me. "You are. I don't know when I've come across a man so beautiful."

"I bet you've come across a few," I quipped. "I'm not all that." I stared at the floor.

"Come on, now. Take a compliment graciously. You deserve it." He paused for a moment, and I could see the wheels turning in his head. He eased a little more toward me when he said, "I've noticed that about you—you're very reluctant to accept any kind of compliment." He cocked his head. "Why do you think that is?"

The question, here in the relative still and dark night, was a sting to my heart—it hit close to home. Why indeed? Could it be that I didn't love myself enough to believe a person when they said something flattering? Was it cynicism or self-loathing that I couldn't simply be grateful for a compliment? I felt a sharp and sudden ache for the little boy inside—one who had grown up being bullied and teased, one who believed the bullies were right and he was less than.

And...that was *not* something I wanted to think about right now, not in this perfect romantic moment.

"Ah, I'm just modest," I said. To deflect further compliments and my own introspection, I told him to "just kiss me."

And he did.

Soon, we were making enough noise that we needed to roll up the windows. Soon, those very same windows were misted over, and our lovely view, outside anyway, was lost in a kind of Brigadoon-like fog. Soon, we reclined the two bucket seats, and our clothes were in heaps behind them. Soon, Walt positioned himself awkwardly but effectively between my legs. Soon, my feet rested on the ceiling.

Soon, we were both crying out in extended bliss.

And all too soon...it was over, leaving us wrung out and heaving.

We parted reluctantly, with awkward, shy smiles. We'd been like two animals that had coupled. Strike that. We actually *were* two animals who had coupled—rather savagely too.

Unlike an animal, though, I had enough presence of mind (and knowledge of British vernacular) to be grateful that I had been royally shagged in a compact car on the banks of the River Avon.

I never could have predicted it!

Every bit as awkward as our lovemaking was the aftermath. We cleaned up as best we could with the fast-food napkins Walt had in his glove compartment. We managed to get ourselves dressed. We rolled down the windows once more, and I imagined a cloud of sex funk drifting out of the windows to stretch over the river.

"Will you still love me tomorrow?" I asked.

Walt got my song reference and said back, "Oh, Carole, you know I will." He stared out the front window, which was at last beginning to regain its transparency. He cleared his throat. "But you know I have to leave tomorrow. I'm supposed to go to Wales if I want to keep on track with my tour."

My afterglow followed the cloud of sex funk right out the window and into the night air. I didn't want him to leave, despite Teddy's charms, despite the touristy plans we had for Bath, despite the prospect of meeting the family that had spawned a creature as unique as Boutros.

Gear shift sticking into my side, I cuddled closer to Walt, my head on his shoulder. "Are you sure? I was hoping we could do a bit of sightseeing. Jane Austen's house, I hear, is around here somewhere. And the buns with clotted cream and strawberry jam at Sally Lunn's are supposed be beyond belief. Life changing."

Walt leered. "I doubt her buns could compare to yours."

"Ah, come on! And thank you. But I do wish you could stay."

Walt let out a sigh; I couldn't discern if it was contented or annoyed. The self-loathing part of me, of course, went with annoyed. That part of me said, "There you go again. Too clingy! You can't just let things be and be grateful for what you have. No, you have to push people away with your worries about commitment and what comes next." Fortunately, I wasn't totally damaged and did allow for the possibility that his sigh was a contented one.

That other part of me gave me permission to stretch out our silence for a while, resisting the urge to ask for more—however we wanted to define "more" in that moment.

At last, Walt turned to me and said, "You know, I really don't need to leave *so* very early. Perhaps we could spend the morning together? A bit of the afternoon?"

Inside, I was jumping up and down and grinning like a chimpanzee with a pile of bananas. But I managed, with mighty reserve, to allow only a small smile. "Really? That would be great."

And we made plans to meet up the following morning at Teddy and Philip's apartment. I already knew what was on the agenda for Boutros, Teddy, and Philip. They were going to get up early and head out to a nearby attraction, Wookey Hole, a series of caverns that Boutros wanted to take his son, Daryl, to. Of course, I was included in that trip and was actually looking forward to it.

I would have to get out of it now because I looked forward *more* to Walt coming over to the apartment after everyone had gone. I was already imagining the luxury of having him, a bed, and several hours of uninterrupted time.

"Sweetheart, I need to get some rest. Can I drop you off somewhere?"

I longed for him to spend the night with me. Maybe that would happen sometime during this trip? I dared not think about a time *after* this trip. I knew when I was going back but hadn't had the courage to ask how long Walt planned on staying here, or if there was another leg to his travel that would include other European countries.

I knew so little about him, really.

We drove in silence to the apartment building, taking several wrong turns because even at best, my sense of direction was lousy. But we managed to get there.

When we were in front of the building, I put a hand on Walt's knee. "Sorry about getting you lost—twice."

"Three times."

We laughed.

Walt shook his head. "In my book, really, there's no such thing as getting lost. It's only a chance to see more. See something wonderful. People travel with too many agendas and schedules. I like to wander, see what life throws my way."

"I like that," I said softly. I leaned across the center console and kissed him deeply. Our tongues dueled, and we heated up again quickly. But then I had a vision of Boutros looking out the window at a little car parked in front, rocking on its axis.

I pressed a hand to Walt's chest. "If I could, I'd ask you to come up. But Boutros and I are staying with a couple. And it's only a tiny one bedroom." I raised my eyebrows. "But that bedroom should be available to us in the morning."

That got a smile out of Walt. "Then so it shall be." He kissed me again—quickly, softly. "Good night."

I opened the passenger door. "Sleep tight. Sweet dreams."

As I was about to exit, Walt placed a hand over mine. "I know I'll dream of you."

I looked back at him, smiling uncertainly.

"You're all I think about since I first found you on that street in Bath. It stands to reason that my subconscious is filled with you."

Sweet as this sentiment was, it also caused a smidgen of worry. I think it was more common sense than my inability to graciously take a compliment that told me Walt was going a bit overboard.

We hadn't known each other long at all. And while I would agree there was some magic happening, I'd also learned that caution wasn't such a bad thing when it came to new relationships. And we couldn't really even say we had a relationship. Not yet!

Maybe I was just exhausted and yearning desperately for sleep. Maybe my head was speaking to me over my heart.

Whatever it was, something told me it was time to say good night, once and for all. Tomorrow, and whatever would come after tomorrow, would help me determine if this magic was real—or if it was two sets of hormones, calling to each other in the night, on holiday.

I squeezed Walt's hand and let go. "I'll see you in the morning. Why don't you plan on around ten? That way, we can be sure to have the place to ourselves."

We kissed once more. I slipped out of the car and stood on the sidewalk, watching Walt drive away. I wondered where he was going.

I wondered where *we* were going.

Chapter Eight

"Oh honey, I could lie here all day," Walt lazily stroked my hair and then got up on one elbow to plant a kiss on my forehead.

We lay together on Teddy and Philip's bed. The sun warmed the sheets as much as the aftereffect of Walt's and my lovemaking. The day outside was clear. Through the open window came the whoosh of traffic and bird cries. The sunlight fell in golden slats across the white linen tangled around our limbs. I imagined us as a Herb Ritts poster or the cover of the *Advocate* magazine, both images in black and white, playing up the brightness and the shadows.

My afterglow, though, was a bit harshed by Walt's wish to laze here all day. I couldn't imagine such a possibility without also letting in the reality that Boutros would eventually walk in on us, trailed by Teddy and Philip. "What have we here?" he might ask, feigning wonder. "Little Miss Mary Poppins got her cherry popped—for the hundredth time."

And yet another red-faced moment would occur.

"A day in bed. Wouldn't that be nice?" I snuggled closer to Walt, nestling my head in the crook between his chin and shoulder. "If only I could wave a magic wand and make it so..."

Walt reached down to give my own magic wand a little squeeze. It lifted its head at the attention, ready to proudly wave once more. But I didn't know how long my friends would be gone.

I laughed. "Nice as this is, we should get up, get ready, get out. We have places to go, buns to eat."

"Mmm..." Walt caressed me, moving his hand from my cock to my ass. "Yes, indeed."

I could tell we wavered dangerously close to a fire being ignited once more. And as much as I yearned for those flames, I yearned even more not to be caught in a compromising position with Walt.

With a mighty display of will, I managed to untangle myself from him and the lovely warm sheets and sit up. "Shall we shower together?"

"They actually have a shower?" Walt asked.

"They do. All the modern conveniences. Come on!" I hopped from the bed.

We headed for the shower with me promising myself over and over, "I will not drop the soap. I will not drop the soap."

I looked back at Walt and thought, *Well, maybe.*

*

"Oh my God." I savored the sweet spreading out over my taste buds. "This is the best thing I've ever eaten."

We were in Sally Lunn's Historic Eating House, enjoying their signature home-baked buns with strawberry jam and clotted cream. As I savored the light bun, tasting something like a cross between bread, brioche, and cake, I took in the place we were sitting.

"This has literally been here for hundreds of years," Walt told me. "It's probably older than anything in America—at least older than anything the colonists brought over." He was cutting his bun with knife and fork, as the waitress had instructed us curtly. She'd probably seen her share of American tourists try to lift the big buns and devour them by hand, like dogs.

I know that's what I would have done had I not been instructed otherwise.

Once we'd finished up, Walt asked, "So what do you want to do now? Check out the Jane Austen house? Go to some of the secondhand bookshops I've seen?" He had a little twinkle in his eye as he offered his last option, "Or take an idyllic drive in the countryside?"

I smiled. "You had me at countryside. Since we don't have a car, it might be my only chance."

"Good. There's a ton of history around here. And more scenery than you can shake a stick at. And we couldn't have asked for better weather." Walt signaled our waitress for our check. When she brought it, he insisted on paying.

I started to argue, but he held up his hand. "Let me treat, okay? Just be grateful to receive."

"Oh, okay. Thank you."

As we headed out on winding country roads and glorious green rolling hills with flowers in bloom, Walt popped a cassette in. An almost otherworldly voice filled the car. It was so beautiful that I closed my eyes, breathing in the aural magic. The female voice might have been speaking directly to me, and I imagined it accompanied by celestial light. I felt surrounded, calm, and embraced.

We hit a pothole, and I opened my eyes, jerked back to reality. I gestured toward the dash. "What is this?"

Walt turned up the music a bit. "*Canticles of Ecstasy.*"

"Wow. Aptly named." The music haunted me, taking me to a different place. I couldn't recall ever hearing such beauty.

"It's the music of Hildegarde von Bingen. She was a medieval nun, and her visions inspired it. These canticles have been around for hundreds of years."

"Really? It's gorgeous. Absolutely stunning."

The music segued into our next destination, an old church in Bradford-on-Avon. As we pulled up outside the tall, narrow gray building, I noticed that there were only a few small windows. It was very simple, yet its obvious age lent it a kind of dignified majesty.

"It looks positively ancient." The stone edifice was near crumbling. Weather had done more than its fair share of aging. Still, the church looked solid and strong.

"It is." Walt shut off the car and turned to regard the church. "It's St. Laurence's. From what I could put together out of one of my travel guides, it dates back roughly to the eleventh century, but some sources say it could go back even further—maybe even seventh century."

"Amazing." The church had a quiet, almost regal beauty. Stately. An almost spiritual vibration emanated from it. I wondered about the people who had passed through its doors over the many years of its lifespan. It radiated a quiet spirituality that I could feel.

We stared for a while. It seemed words could do St. Laurence's no justice. All around us, it was quiet. No other people. No other cars.

Walt broke the silence. "Want to go inside?"

I was surprised. I didn't think seeing the interior would be an option. "Is it open?"

Walt shrugged. "It should be. They generally don't lock these houses of worship up."

"I'd love to see. If we can."

"Let's go."

We got out of the car. It was no problem getting into the church. Inside, we walked quietly because the place was so calm and serene. It was very simple and gray but still gave off a sense of majesty.

Reverent, we found a pew and sat. Light streamed in through the small windows. I looked around, expecting a priest or maybe a nun.

But the place was deserted.

Just as I was bowing my head, thinking I might return to my Catholic roots and say an Our Father or a Hail Mary to be polite, I noticed Walt looking around out of the corner of my eye. I got the sense he was checking to see if the coast was clear.

He grinned. And then he reached for my fly.

"What are you doing?" I whispered, frantic. I swiveled my head around to make sure no one else had entered the church in the last three seconds.

He fingered the button holding together my jeans.

"You have got to be kidding me," I said. Still, I didn't make any move to stop him.

With a deft flick of a couple of fingers, he had the button undone. And then, just as fast, he had my fly down. I'd not worn anything under my jeans, and my dick, hard despite the reverential atmosphere, popped up. My dick doesn't recognize whether it's in a church or a bathhouse. If there's a good-looking man nearby, it responds. I suppose you could make a case for this being as the Good Lord intended.

Walt grabbed it and gave it a playful squeeze. "There should be a chorus of angels singing," he said softly. "And a shaft of pearly white light shining down on it."

"You're terrible," I whispered. I knew the right thing to do was to knock his hand away and mention that we were in a house of God. But I couldn't find the words. All the blood from my brain seemed to be rushing south. All I could imagine was the feel of Walt's mouth around my engorged cock, surrounding it with velvet wetness.

Imagination turned to reality in about five seconds flat. Walt's head made like a cow lowering its head to graze, and very soon, my eyelids were at half-mast as his head bobbed up and down on my crotch.

There was no other word for it. The sensations were *heavenly*. So heavenly, in fact, that within less than a minute or two, I was filling Walt's mouth with my seed.

"Take this all of you and eat it," I whispered.

Walt moved his head up to reveal my still throbbing dick. A line of come ran down the shaft. "For this is your body." He wiped an errant drop of jizz off his mustache with the back of his hand. "And your body's delicious."

Without another word, sacrilegious or otherwise, Walt pulled out his own engorged member and quickly jerked himself off. I watched in horror, lust, and awe as he shot a big load on the stone floor.

"We've got to get out of here," I said.

If we weren't caught by a priest making the rounds, we would surely be struck by a bolt of celestial lightning if we lingered much longer.

We were damned.

We pulled up, zipped up, and kissed.

Holding hands, we exited our Saxon church. I'd like to add that we skipped, but that would be stretching the truth.

I was giddy with relief, afterglow, and a sense that my Catholic relatives would want to have me burned at the stake if they could see me now.

*

Walt dropped me off at the apartment building about an hour later. We sat in the car for a while, not talking but simply enjoying the contentment of having the other nearby. I've always thought that the quality of a relationship can be measured by its silences. If you can sit with each other without the pressure of always needing to speak, this could be a relationship that might weather the test of time. Besides, people don't give enough import to what can often be said in silences.

Reluctantly, I at last broke the quiet. "Thank you for a very, um, unique day. As Sophie Tucker would say, 'I'll never forget it, ya know.'"

Walt chuckled.

"No, I mean it. I'm sure I'll never forget you because you're the man who sucked me off in an eleventh-century Saxon church. I very much doubt I'll ever have that experience again."

"Unless it's with me."

"Unless it's with you." I smiled. "Are you thinking of staying longer?" I asked hopefully, wondering what other religious monuments we could desecrate. I was already beginning to wonder how I might ask Boutros if he would mind terribly if I left him for a few days to throw in my lot with Walt.

Walt shook his head. "No, I can't. I really want to head down to Wales. Never been."

I hoped he'd ask me to join him. I was ready to say yes. I waited, but no invitation came.

"Well, I hope to see you again."

"And I you, Ricky." He touched my cheek.

We stared into one another's eyes for a moment. Would this just be a summer holiday romance, to morph gradually into a bittersweet memory of what once was? Would I look back on my time with Walt one day with both a sense of gratitude and wondering what might have been? Should I bury my impulse to try to control this moment and simply let it be?

"Well, just so you know, we're here for a couple more days and then we head back to London for a few days before flying back to America."

"Have you been to Boston?" Walt asked.

"No. It's one big American city I've never visited, except through hanging out with the regulars at Cheers." I grinned.

"Well, maybe you can come up and see me sometime. I'd love to show you around. I have a friend who has a gorgeous place up in New Hampshire; we could head up there for the weekend. It's a big secluded house with a pool, and we'd have it all to ourselves."

"That would be amazing. I'd love that." I wondered how I could afford it and when I could find the time, since I'd used up all of my vacation days for the year on this very trip. I'd find a way, even if I had to quit my job. I was thinking of going freelance anyway.

Walt groped around in the glove compartment until he found a small spiral-bound notebook. He wrote down his home phone and home address, along with his email. I took it and returned the favor.

"I'm glad you see a bit of a future for us."

"We can't see what the future holds," Walt said. "But I do hope you're in mine, Ricky."

"Me too." I had to bite my tongue from asking if he was sure he couldn't stay. "I guess I should be getting inside."

Walt gave me a long kiss. "And I guess I should be hitting the road."

"You drive very well on the left side."

"Thanks."

We looked at each other for a long moment. Despite the exchange of contact information, I really wasn't sure we'd see each other again. Yes, I felt a shiny bit of limerence for this man. Yes, I desperately wanted to see us together somewhere in the future. But I was jaded enough to know that moments like this promised nothing. If I had a nickel for every guy I'd brought home from the bars in Chicago, thinking the next morning as I smiled sleepily at him over pancakes at Buddy's that we might have a future and then never hearing a word again, I'd be a rich man, traveling first class.

So I tempered my expectations. My head sang a Doris Day song to my heart, "Que Sera, Sera." And my heart almost bought it. Almost.

"Bye, Walt. Have fun on the rest of your journey. And I hope you meet *no one* like me."

"I hope so too."

I got out of the car and turned to give a small wave. I watched Walt drive away, trying to hold on to the belief that we'd be together again, that he wouldn't meet someone else on some street in Wales, someone with whom he'd exchange a mouthful of beer.

Chapter Nine

"I'm worn out." I glanced over at Boutros next to me on the train.

"Color me surprised, kitten." Boutros's voice was loaded with sarcasm. "We should probably have gotten you some Depends. I'm sure your rectum is all but prolapsed."

I rolled my eyes. You might be asking yourself, "This is his best friend? I'd hate to see what an enemy looks like."

"Come on, be nice." I stared out at the summer day flashing by in shades of blue, yellow, green.

We were headed back to London for three more days.

"Be nice? And what would that accomplish? Then I'd simply be like everyone else in your dreadful life. Mediocre." Boutros belied his words with a kind smile. He really didn't need to. I knew his cruel barbs meant that he loved me—character assassination, snide remarks, and bald cruelty had been our way of communicating through all the years we'd known each other. It was the currency of our affection. I'd be worried if Boutros *wasn't* being unkind.

"You're right. I'd probably hate you. Well, at least more than I already do." I returned his kind smile, sweetening it even more.

"We had quite a time, didn't we?" Boutros patted my hand.

"Oh, honey, that's for sure. And you don't even know everything I did!" I'd yet to tell him about the buggery on the River Avon and the blasphemous fellatio performed at St. Laurence's. Somehow, I liked having these secrets to myself. Keeping them hidden away made them somehow more precious.

"I have to commend you."

"For what?"

Boutros was quiet for a moment. "For keeping your hands off Teddy. Thank you. I don't know what I would have done if you'd slept with him. I suspect this little trip would have been over at that point. And I would have loved you no more. There's only so much sluttiness I can tolerate before I draw a line."

"Your concerns aside, I don't know what *Philip* would have done." There'd been some tension in the little apartment, especially yesterday afternoon, when I took off my shirt in front of everyone in the living room in preparation for heading into the shower. Honest to God, the removal of my shirt was *not* meant to be provocative. But hell, I might as well have had a stripping soundtrack as far as Teddy was concerned. His eyes practically bulged, and I suspect he barely held in the drool. Somewhere in his imagination, Oscar Peterson was playing "Night Train" on his piano. Teddy seemed ready to cry out, "Take it off! Take it all off!"

Instead, he said, "Ooh, look at all that fur!" He pointed to my mat of dark chest hair. "Lovely."

As much as I did adore the way British men were always calling everything lovely, I tried to gloss over his compliment by asking where we were going to dinner that night. It was Teddy's birthday, and he wanted a proper celebration.

"Shoes of the Fisherman," Philip said, eyes shooting daggers toward me. "Good seafood. No chips." He grinned as though he knew this would disappoint the lowly Yank his husband was obviously lusting for.

We'd had a lovely dinner, with Teddy insisting that I have a pudding at the end. That's when I discovered that even an apple tart was "pudding" in British vernacular.

When we got home, Boutros and Philip went outside to smoke, and it was then Teddy proposed a quickie.

"Just let me suck you off."

I never thought I'd refuse a blow job, but I pushed him away because he was standing too close. I could smell the garlic from his shrimp scampi on his breath. "It wouldn't be right."

"Philip won't mind." He chuckled. "We have an understanding." He reached for my zipper.

"Maybe Philip won't mind, but I would. I'm kind of seeing that guy I went off with."

"Oh, please. Be a mate. It's my birthday."

"Then you should have my cock," I said, a little bitterly.

It was then Boutros and Philip had returned. Teddy and I quickly retreated to different corners of the room, him guilty and me not so much.

*

Now, on the train, I looked back at the memory and my restraint with some fondness. I didn't know I had it in me.

Other memories of the trip rose to the surface of my consciousness.

I'd never forget meeting Boutros's mother and father. They lived on what he called a "council estate" on a hill overlooking Bath. The location was quite bucolic and an ode to the color green. Miles of it, in all its different variations.

Boutros's parents, who called him Bertie, were polar opposites. His father was a big, affable man with a walrus mustache and a thick head of snow-white hair. He made me feel immediately at home, taking me off with him to give me a tour of the small stone house and its tiny cramped rooms. "We only had Bertie," he said. "Just the one. After the likes of him, Mum and me couldn't handle the idea of any more." He guffawed, and I joined him, complicit in understanding. I could imagine Boutros presented his fair share of challenges growing up.

We went outside so Dad could show me his vegetable garden. I feigned interest in the patches of herbs, tomatoes, and courgettes but could hear Boutros and his mother bickering shrilly inside the whole time.

His mother had all but ignored me when we came in the door. She had fangs and claws, sharpened and bared for her little boy.

The visit was uncomfortable, something out of an Edward Albee play.

I never did find out what the mother-son sniping was about, so I took this quiet opportunity on the train now to find out.

"Oh, I told her there was only one thing of mine I wanted from my boyhood in the house, and she wouldn't let me have it."

I imagined it was something valuable, or something the couple currently weren't using.

Boutros said, "It was my stuffed monkey. I called him Charlie, and I slept with him every night."

I wanted to burst into laughter, but when I saw the hurt expression on Boutros's face, the longing, despair, and pain, I quickly sucked my mirth back inside.

"She said I could have anything I wanted in the house, anything but Charlie." Boutros caught my gaze, and I don't think I'd ever seen him look so stricken. I wanted to take him in my arms, but we were not the type of friends who hugged. "She knew that monkey was the only thing I wanted. That's why she wouldn't let me have it."

I understood. Withholding something Boutros held dear gave her power over him, even though he was a grown man who no longer even lived in her country.

"When we bury her, it's going to be facedown."

"Why?"

"So when she tries to claw her way out of the grave, which she will inevitably do, she'll be digging down instead of up."

I was suddenly grateful for my own mother back in Ohio, who made me and my sisters the focus of her life and love.

I had to mentally shift gears, so I reminded Boutros of the couple we'd seen walking near Bath Abbey, the gorgeous Anglican church overlooking the Avon.

"Remember what we saw there?"

"Oh God!" Boutros grabbed my arm, and we both collapsed into giggles, loud enough to cause some of our fellow travelers to turn in their seats and stare.

It was around sunset, and we'd seen a lovely young couple emerge from the greenery around the Abbey, holding hands and looking oh-so-romantic. An accurate portrait of *afterglow*.

The warm and fuzzy image was marred by the fact that the back of her skirt had been hastily, and mistakenly, tucked into her panties.

We'd laughed then too and debated whether we should let her know. After all, she was walking down one of Bath's main streets in a most embarrassing fashion, pun intended.

Bless her heart.

In the end, we decided not to. To warn her would be to ruin the story she and her beau might later tell their grandchildren when they grew old enough to understand outdoor sex in public places. Who knew? Maybe the forbear of one of those very grandchildren had just been conceived in the shadow of Bath Abbey.

We'd laughed until tears came as we'd waited for this very train on the platform. Boutros had found an issue of the British humor magazine *Viz* in one of the bookstores. The two of us, with our in-common sick senses of humor, guffawed until we were almost breathless at the comic-strip antics of the Fat Slags, most of which usually revolved around one or the other of them caught "'avin' a shit" at the most inopportune time. Back in Chicago, these gals were the type Boutros and I liked to pal around with.

There was also an extended description of the kinky sex taking place inside a pet store, among the animals. The article had as its capper, "And then I shat in his beak." The line nearly made us both pee our pants.

I looked over at Boutros now. He'd fallen asleep, and his mouth was open, a small line of drool escaping onto his goatee. Instead of being repulsed, as I usually was when looking at him, I was oddly charmed, like a mother looking at her sleeping babe—if that babe smoked cigarettes and offered up his bum for the licking to any number of lusty innkeepers.

Snickering, I relaxed, easing back into the seat and letting my limbs go soft under the gentle rocking motion of the train.

I thought of Walt and imagined him on a Boston street. I'd never been to Boston, so I brought to mind the image of a cobblestone street, bordered by trees and brownstone apartment houses, at the end of which would be a line of blue—the Atlantic Ocean.

Would we see each other once we'd returned to America, or was that only wishful thinking?

The lingering disappointment over that realistically not happening had little to do with Walt and more to do with me.

I was now in my midthirties and could honestly say I'd never really been in love. Not truly. Oh sure, there'd been men (and a woman!) I'd cared deeply about and harbored hopes for long-term coupling with, but the actual feeling of *being in love* remained a mystery. I wondered if the capacity for romantic love was simply out of my reach, if I'd been born without the gene for it.

I had once despaired over this with the woman with whom I'd shared most everything because she seemed to care more than anyone else in the world about my happiness—my mom. She'd told me, when I asked her what true love felt like, "I don't know that I can put the feeling into words, Ricky. I don't know that I'd want to. It's kind of good it being something you can't really describe, like that peculiar feeling you get in your gut when someone really attractive walks by." She'd snorted with laughter. "I certainly felt it with your dad, even though he was, and still is, a self-centered son of a bitch who was all wrong for me. If I'd wanted a logically happy life, I should have gone for his brother, Ray."

"But then I wouldn't exist."

"But then you wouldn't exist," she conceded. "But love doesn't work with logic. There has to be a spark." Her eyes looked a little faraway. It was at that moment, I think, that I realized my parents had a life before I was born, that their hopes and dreams were something entirely separate from being my mom or my dad. She looked at me and hastened to add, "But oh, how I love my boy!" And then she, as Sicilian mothers are wont to do, pinched my cheek.

I realized suddenly that the two people I loved most in the world, her and the man snoring softly beside me, had more in common than I would have first credited them with. Both seemed to know me better than I knew myself.

It was also interesting that there was zero erotic component to the two relationships I held most dear. And I wondered why someone like me, who'd lost count of the number of sexual partners I'd had, loved most the people for whom anything sexual was completely out of the question.

Would I ever be able to unite sex and love? Isn't that the path most people followed?

Sorry, Boutros, sweetie, my heart, but it's true—the notion of sex with you has all the appeal of having sex with dear old Mom.

If Walt and I did see each other on American shores, I wondered if something could possibly come of the relationship apart from fantastic orgasms that would become less and less fantastic the more of them we shared. Yes, folks, that's the way my sex life worked. I suspected this was the sad truth for most of my brothers and sisters on this fine planet we called home. The sex always decreased in pleasure and excitement. And yet I always seemed to be looking for that initial thrill, over and over. Drug addicts called the phenomenon "chasing the dragon." I chased it but seemed doomed to chase it with a different dragon almost every time.

I closed my eyes with the thought that, despite my cynicism in matters related to true love, I was still young enough, eager enough, and naïve enough to believe it could happen.

And it could happen to me.

And Walt.

But the real question was—would it happen to us both at the same time?

Chapter Ten

We were back in London, and strangely, it felt like home. The winding streets of Westminster with its closely spaced buildings, the stately watch of Big Ben, the green of St. James's Park, the hustle and bustle of it all as yet another generation of Londoners hurried home to their tea or to the pub or simply to stroll along the Thames.

I felt almost like one of them as Boutros and I made our way to Trevor's flat, dragging our suitcases behind us. Boutros had the keys in his pocket as Trevor had left the country for Spain on his own holiday. Most likely I would never see our kind host again.

In fact I was feeling so British, I thought I'd try out an accent. I'd been listening for so long that I thought it would fairly trip off my tongue.

"Fancy a kebab before we get home? Maybe do a takeaway? Wouldn't that be nice?"

Boutros stopped in the street to stare at me. He narrowed his eyes. "Who *are* you?"

"Your mate, Ricky."

Boutros made a *tsk* noise and shook his head. "Listen, if you think you sound remotely British, you've another think coming. Trying to ape the accent makes you sound even more dreadfully American than you already are, so quit it." He turned abruptly and kept walking.

I followed, mumbling, "I'll take that as a no on the kebab, then."

*

That night, Boutros had a date of sorts. Not a romantic one, but to meet up with a fellow compatriot in the creation of art—a cartoonist who had enjoyed some success on this side of the pond. His visions of a pair of gay Peter Pans, everyone knowing they were well past their prime but themselves, had been syndicated in gay newspapers across Europe.

He and Boutros, brought together through the magic of mutual friends plus email, had corresponded over the years. Tonight was Boutros's first chance to meet him, live and in the flesh. Because there was the possibility this could morph from a casual meetup into an erotic encounter, I was not invited, which was fine with me.

As much as I loved Boutros, I needed some time alone. Introverts are born that way. Too much proximity to people for whom we even have great affection tends to drain us. My tank was empty.

So once he'd left, in his muslin shirt and ripped jeans, I took a bubble bath and dressed casually for an evening out in a pair of gray button-fly Levi's and a red Chicago Bulls T-shirt from which I had artfully cut the sleeves. I thought the ensemble, paired with a three-day growth of dark beard and my Nikes, made me look sporty and butch, despite the nelly queen hiding in the shadows.

There was a pub not far along on the subway line called the Royal Vauxhall. Boutros had mentioned their drag shows being legendary and that the place attracted a good crowd on almost every night of the week.

The promise of alcohol and entertainment, surrounded by gay peers, was welcoming to me. The old Ricky would have once gone along thinking he'd find a sexy stranger with whom to spend the night (okay, or five minutes in a bathroom stall), exploring each other's nooks and crannies with heedless abandon.

But meeting Walt had changed me, had put my taste for anonymous sex on hold. Temporarily? Who knew? All I did know was that the promise of being able to disappear into a crowd, where the focus was not on the next pretty boy but a raucous drag queen on a stage, seemed comforting and appealed to the introvert in me.

Hadn't someone once said that we are never more alone than when in the midst of a crowd? If we want, we can disappear into a crowd.

I set out into the night, just as dusk was beating a hasty retreat, leaving the sky above London a palette of gray and lavender, tinged at the top with darkness and the first few stars beginning to emerge.

As I headed toward the station at St. James's, I passed through a little park, as opposed to the big park for which the Tube station had been named. This was a tiny city park on a corner—a few trees, a few benches, a little green, some litter, a pigeon-shit-ornamented statue of some battle hero whom no one remembered.

Intent on getting to the station, and more than a little worried that I might get lost forever in the London underground labyrinth, I heard someone call out my name as I passed by. At first I didn't stop, because among the millions of people in London, who would know me by name?

The voice sounded again, louder. "Ricky?"

I stopped and turned around, peering into the gloom of the park. There was a male figure sitting on a bench, but I couldn't really make him out well because he was hidden in shadow cast by the leaves of the tree above him.

The orange sodium-vapor glow of the streetlight didn't reach him.

Cautiously, I made my way toward him. And when I was within a couple feet of him, those features that I so loved shaped themselves into a familiar and welcome image.

"Walt. It's you." I shook my head. "You seem to have a bit of magic in you." I sat down close, our shoulders touching. God, I didn't know how much I'd wanted to see him again until I actually did.

"How's that?"

"You turn up in the most surprising ways. If I didn't know better, I'd say you were following me. Or that I had the power of wish fulfillment."

"Well, since actually following you would be almost impossible, what with me traveling by car and you by train, let's just consider the possibility that fate is keeping our paths crossing. And maybe..." He placed a hand on my cheek to turn my face toward his and leaned in for a quick kiss. "Maybe you and I being together again is exactly what the universe has planned for us."

I knew what Boutros would think of such a line, how he would scoff at it. But I was charmed by the idea that something beautifully strange and wonderful in the world kept bringing us back together.

As though it were meant to be.

I pulled away. We were in public, and we were still years away from when two men kissing in a public park would be acceptable by everyone, if it ever would be. I said softly, "I'm so glad to see you. This is a surprise I didn't even allow myself to entertain."

"It was meant to be, sweetheart."

The fact that he called me sweetheart caused a little chill to pass through me, a tingle like an electric shock. And then I felt warm.

Were things meant to be? Was there a grand plan for all of us?

"What happened to Wales? I thought you were headed down there for a while."

He smiled, staring off for a moment into the darkness. "I started that way, but instead of focusing on the simple beauty of that countryside, I couldn't get the simple beauty of you lying naked on sun-drenched sheets in London out of my head."

"Oh, you are so corny. So full of shit." I frowned.

"There you go again, unable to take a simple compliment. Whether you know it or not, you are a beautiful man and quite capable of worming your way into a guy's head and staying there. The truth is I thought I could escape you, but you're like an earworm. The harder I tried not to think about you, the more prominent you became in my thoughts." He shrugged and went on, "I knew you were coming back to London, knew in general where you were staying, and, of course, I have my trump card."

He reached into his back pocket and took out his worn leather wallet. From it, he extracted a little slip of paper. "Ta-da. The phone number you gave me for the friend you're staying with. I was going to call in the morning."

"You were?" I felt delight that even I had to admit was a little out of proportion. He was just a man, for Christ's sake.

"I was. I was going to call and see if I could interest you in a proper fry-up."

"Fried eggs, bacon, sausages, tomato, mushrooms," I rattled off what I could remember.

"Exactly. But obviously fate had other plans in store for us. It didn't want us to wait so long." He took my hand and, understanding my reticence about public displays of affection, held it out of sight beneath the wood slats of the bench upon which we were sitting. "You look nice. Were you off to the pubs?"

I thought I could see a little weakness around his lips, perhaps even a little fear. Then it dawned on me. "You're not jealous, are you?"

He shook his head, and I spotted the lie as easily as I could see the neon sign across the way from us, advertising Cornish pasties.

"Yeah, I was headed out to a drag show, a few pints."

Walt let go of my hand. "I should let you go."

"Oh no!"

He smiled. "Maybe you want a little company? I've yet to see a drag show over here. Let's go see how the Brits do it."

"I sincerely doubt they do it much different than us Americans. Men gusseted and corseted. Tons of eye shadow and mascara. Lip gloss for days. Sequins. And lip-synching to Gloria Gaynor or Liza Minelli. Besides, I have a better idea." I thought of the empty flat and of Boutros telling me not to wait up for him.

"Oh?" Walt's grin was joyful...and a little wicked. "I'm so glad because I'm at a youth hostel. No privacy whatsoever."

"So let's go." And I took his hand to lead him away.

I wasn't about to be daunted by, and certainly not judged by, the court of public opinion. It was a dangerous thought, but what the hell? If someone didn't like the sight of two men holding hands, that was their problem, not ours.

Still, I hoped the two of us would make it back to Trevor's flat intact.

I had plans in store for us, and they required us being, er, well, intact.

*

I opened the door to the flat to reveal slatted beams of light falling across the carpeted floor. I liked to think of them as moonbeams gone expressionistic, but they were just the light seeping in between Trevor's cheap mini blinds, half-open. There was a kind of noirish beauty to the image.

I also imagined that Walt and I were a couple, returning to our home after a constitutional around the neighborhood. This place could be the apartment we'd moved into shortly after we'd first met on a street in Brighton. We'd moved in together much too soon, against all reason, but we'd done it anyway because it felt so right. And now our home was as comfortable as a pair of old slippers.

We'd lived and loved here long enough to be totally at ease—television and bowls of ice cream in the evenings. Bickering in the morning over who got to use the bathroom first. The endless debate over whether we should get a dog or a cat.

A happy, homely domestic life played out in moments, even though it was years long, fashioned from holidays, tears, laughter, and caresses. It made me both sad and warm at the same time.

And the best part was that we were *not* such an old couple that the fires within us had died down much. There was still a lot of passion. And even if we were an old couple, we defied the odds, still finding each other thrilling even after many years together.

But the passion wasn't hard to fake, or fake at all, really, because it was here in spades, like a third presence in the darkened room. I couldn't wait to feel Walt's naked skin against my own.

I turned and, through the gloom, saw him reaching for the light switch.

"No," I said softly. "Leave it off. I don't feel like light. I don't feel like talking."

Wisely, Walt made no response at all, other than a small sigh, as he leaned against the front door, waiting for me to make my next move.

I took his hand and led him through the living room, past the bath, and into the bedroom.

Here, the curtains remained open, and a blinking light across the street repeated "Chemists" over and over. Tonight I was not feeling exhibitionistic, as I had in Brighton, so I pulled the draperies closed.

The room was bathed in almost complete darkness.

Now, know this about me—up until this point I had not been a fan of sex in the dark. The thought of it seemed puritanical, steeped in shame, a way of hiding. I'd always liked all the lights. I wanted to see what I was getting. I liked bearing witness to a man thrusting above me, watching his desire peak, observing his features contorting as he surrendered to ecstasy.

There was something about this darkness tonight that simply felt right. As it melted and our eyes adjusted, I could just make out Walt's tall frame, standing close. It was as though he'd stepped out of an old black-and-white movie, bathed in silver.

And what was more romantic than that?

"Undress for me," I said, my words coming out somehow stronger in the shadows that had gathered in the room.

I watched as he slowly peeled off the white button-down shirt that practically glowed, as though it retained the illumination from the street lamps outside. The shadows, rather than hiding the definition of his chest and stomach, defined them, making them stand out. "Everything?" he asked.

"Everything."

He undid the fly of his jeans, button by button, until at last I saw that he, too, had opted to go commando tonight. His cock popped out as though aching for release.

"Shoes too."

He kicked off his sneakers, which disappeared into the gloom in the corners.

At last, he stood naked before me.

"On the bed." I pointed. He backed a little, until the mattress hit him behind the knees. And then, very gracefully, he went over backward on the bed. He lay spread-eagled, and his eyes, staring, glimmered like topaz.

I moved toward him with no intention on my part of removing even one stitch. Tonight had become a night for new things. In the past, I swear I could have won contests if the aim was to see who could get undressed the quickest. I was usually out of all of my clothes at only the slightest provocation.

But tonight, perversely perhaps, I could imagine nothing sexier than me, fully clothed, with a man, fully naked.

I knelt between his spread legs and began by worshipping his feet.

A lot happened that night, and much of it was new. Darkness. The wonderful contrast of being clothed while my partner was naked. And me topping Walt at last.

I guess I did have to remove a bit of clothing, after all.

*

When it was over and we lay gasping on top of the plaid comforter, our eyes making of the room a movie set from the 1940s, Walt said, "I hate to go all the way back to the hostel."

"Are you really staying in a youth hostel?"

"Well, it's actually a dorm room at the London School of Economics. They rent them out when school's not in full session to poor travelers like me." He grinned. "But it's all the way over in Islington, a long train journey by night. Who knows what could happen to me? I could be beaten or raped."

"I think you just were."

"Oh, honey, no, you can't rape the willing. And I was *very* willing." He smiled.

"I noticed."

He yawned, leaning farther back into the pillows. "My...it's such a long, long way. And who knows how frequently the trains run at this hour. Didn't you say the St. James's station closed at eleven?"

"I said nothing of the sort, but you may be right. You're terrible at hinting. But, as much as I'd like to, I can't let you stay here. My friend shares this bed with me."

"And he's only just a friend." Walt snorted.

"Yes! Yes, there's just the one bed, as you can see. I very much doubt he'll stay out the night, even did he happen to get as lucky as I did."

Walt sat up. "You're really going to force me out into the dangerous big-city night?"

"I really am. But not by choice, Walt. I'd love nothing more than for us to fall asleep in each other's arms."

"Wouldn't that be pretty?"

And just like that, a kind of gloom, not of physical darkness, but of disappointment, fell across the bed. The afterglow winked out like a firefly mistaken for a mosquito and slapped.

Together, without meaning to, we both sighed.

And together again, we both laughed.

Walt swung his legs over the side of the bed. "I have to pee. And then I suppose I should get myself ready to take my leave." He touched my cheek and then hopped out of bed. "Should I say some lines from Romeo and Juliet? About parting being such sweet sorrow?"

"No. Look how they ended up. Go on!" I watched his ass rise and fall as he left the room. He closed the door after him.

I lay on my back, now naked, and contemplated my toes. I listened to the rush of his pee, the too-loud flush of the toilet (which still had a tank above the commode—one flushed it by yanking on a chain).

Surprising myself, I actually drifted off for a minute. In that quick moment, I dreamed that Walt was my husband of many years, returning to our bed to continue our slumber together. Who would make coffee in the morning?

I woke for real as Walt slid in next to me. He pulled the top sheet and comforter over us both and patted it down, making us snug.

"What are you doing?"

"I met your friend."

"What?" Now I was fully awake. I got up on my elbows.

"Boutros. I ran into him as I was coming out of the bathroom. A little odd, but nice. He told me he'd already made up the couch for himself. And that I should stay."

"You're lying."

"He said he came in and heard us going at it like a whore and her trick in an East End alley and thought he better plan on the couch tonight."

"You're not lying." I smiled and relaxed into the pillows. Boutros's wit was as distinctive as his fingerprint.

I relaxed. Maybe I did know what love felt like. I leaned over and kissed Walt good night. "Good night...till it be 'morrow."

I think it was only seconds until I was asleep again and returning to my dream, something that almost never happened.

Chapter Eleven

"Are you sure about this? What if we get caught?" I could just imagine calling Boutros from some London jail, asking him if he had bail money.

And I imagined his response. "Money? No, sweetheart. You'll have to rot in your cell, I'm afraid. It's what you get for not observing posted cautions. But here's the reason not to worry—you'll find a big bruiser to protect you, to make you his bitch, and you'll get that happy-ever-after you've dreamed of."

Walt and I loitered outside the entrance gate to Kew Gardens. It was a large wrought-iron affair with ornamental concrete columns rising up on either side. Walt told me it was called Elizabeth Gate. "After Elizabeth Taylor," he quipped. To the left of the double gates was the entrance to the park, which was clearly closed and locked. Visiting hours were over.

Walt had proposed we find a place where we could slip inside. "No one will know. The park is huge. I'm sure the buildings, like the Temperate House and the Palm House, are locked up. Even if they weren't, it's a safe bet they're patrolled, plus there would be CCTV cameras. But I think we can wander around a bit, sniff some posies, and slip right back out again, with no one the wiser."

I was nervous. I was wiser, or so I liked to believe. Civil disobedience was not my thing. I'd seen the movie *Midnight Express*. I knew what could happen to travelers in foreign countries who got imprisoned. I could imagine long years locked up in the Tower.

I looked around me. It was yet another gorgeous summer night, the air sweet, the sky a deep and almost shocking shade of blue. Couldn't we simply get back on the train and head into London proper? Find a nice restaurant that served a creamy spotted dick?

"Come on," Walt urged. "It'll be fun. And so much more memorable than if we'd gotten in under ordinary circumstances. And look—there's no one around. Not a soul."

It was true. Kew Gardens was quite a ways outside of the city proper. Since it was closed, it was possessed of an almost ghostly emptiness. And I had to admit the idea of sneaking in, illicit and dangerous, did appeal to my dark side.

"I don't know."

"It's not like it'll be the first time today we've done something naughty in one of London's fine public parks." He winked.

That much was true. Earlier that afternoon, we'd been to Kensington Gardens for a picnic and to see the famous Peter Pan statue there.

We'd ended up in a men's toilet, with Walt fucking me from behind in a stall while parkgoers came in and out, having a pee and washing their hands.

My orgasm had been the most silent and intense I think I'd ever had. Having to keep myself quiet simply made it more powerful.

We emerged from our stall looking like two Cheshire cats, I'm sure.

Would there be buggery in Kew Gardens if we dared to sneak in? I doubted it—I was still sore from a few hours ago. Even my well-used asshole deserved a rest now and then, like an overworked maid.

Shaking my head, I told Walt he was incorrigible.

Rightly taking that as a yes, he grabbed my hand, and we wandered around until we found a place where we could slip in. Entrance was surprisingly easy. No alarms went off.

We spent an hour or so amid the lush gardens, feeling like we were the only two people on earth. There was something luxurious in an almost metaphysical way about having the acres of trees, grasses, and flowerbeds all to ourselves. It made me feel more at one with them—it was truly heavenly.

Yet all too soon, darkness began to stain the upper sky, and the sun began its descent to the west. The train journey back to Westminster would be a long one. Reluctantly, we slid out the way we'd come in and headed for the station.

The ride back was quiet, almost as silent as we'd been in the stall at Kensington Gardens, but a lot less delightful. A kind of pensive tension hung in the air between us. I stared out the window, unable to help feeling a sense of loss. I told myself I was only spoiling the last little dribble of time we had together, wasting it by being morose.

It didn't matter. My head got the logic of my argument, but my heart didn't.

When we parted after our adventures that day, my cynicism got up from its seat in the wings and took center stage. I was pretty certain this would be the last time I would see Walt. Holiday flings are just that. This had been a special one, but it was only what it was. The fact that he lived in Boston and me in Chicago, with close to a thousand miles separating us, didn't bode well for our future.

I admit it—I was feeling grim, hopeless. Perhaps I was just tired.

We'd tried to make the most of the day, starting off in the morning at Harrods' food court, then our picnic with Peter Pan, our lust in the loo, our train ride out to Kew Gardens—it had been a very full day. A wonderful day, one of the best of this vacation.

And yet my fatigue was deeper and more pronounced than I thought it had a right to be. It was getting near the end of my time abroad, and all the excitement and newness of my experiences were, perhaps, having a cumulative effect. Part of me was mourning the eventual loss of someone I thought I could love, and the other part wanted to get into bed—alone—and pull the covers over my head.

Maybe some of my malaise was simply due to the fact that I was furious at the universe for denying me romantic love for so long and then delivering it under near-impossible circumstances. Out of the many, many men I met in Chicago, why couldn't one of *them* have stirred the same feelings as Walt had in such a short time?

Sure, I could go all Pollyanna and imagine Walt and I would defy the odds: that ours would be one of those long-distance relationships that didn't wither on the vine as life and new people intervened. Ours could be the one-in-a-million coupling that actually bloomed and flourished, fed by distance instead of destroyed by it.

We arrived at last at St. James's station. There was a cruel, face-saving part of me that simply wanted to hurry off the train without a goodbye or even a backward glance at Walt. A clean cut. It was a silly thought, born from the belief I could somehow spare myself the "sweet sorrow" of parting.

Walt and I ascended to the busy street, dodging commuters as they hurried into and out of the subway station. He pointed to a little restaurant across the street—a grimy diner—and suggested a cup of tea before we headed off our separate ways. "I don't want to say goodbye yet." Walt's smile was sweet and innocent.

Again I wanted to say no. "Oh, all right." I looked down at the sidewalk, where someone had tossed a piece of blue bubblegum.

Walt eyed me. "Wow. Such enthusiasm."

"I'm sorry, Walt." And I really was. "My energy is starting to flag, I think. It's not you."

Silently, we waited for a break in the traffic and crossed the street. As usual, I looked the wrong way, right instead of left, and nearly got a hit by a passing scooter.

Inside the diner, the lights were uncomfortably bright. The linoleum floors and tiled walls looked dingy, besmirched by years of grease. A tinny sound system played Oasis's "Some Might Say." The song was a big hit in the UK that spring and summer.

We both ordered tea, and Walt added a couple of scones to the order. I had absolutely no appetite.

When the tea came, Typhoo in bags with two cups of hot water, Walt laid a hand gently over mine. "Honey, please. You need to tell me what's wrong. It seemed like we were so happy when we left the gardens. Your mood took a nosedive on the way here."

I busied myself dunking my tea bag in and out of the hot water, putting one of the pair of scones on my plate, and staring at it for a moment. It had the same appeal as if I had laid a slug on the plate. I looked around for sugar and saw none on the table. I would have to signal our waitress and ask for it. Fuck it. I didn't care. I wasn't planning on drinking much of the tea anyway.

"That's just it, Walt. I *was* happy. But all too soon I realized you and me—we're a summer fling. Why kid ourselves that this is anything more than that? You're a beautiful man, you're great in bed, you're funny, you're spiritual, you're adventurous, you're kind. But we both know how this story ends. Sure, we'll get home, promise to write and call, maybe even make plans to visit the other, but then life will intrude. You'll meet someone else, or I will. Pressures will mount with work. Seasons will change. Those letters, emails, calls will become fewer and further between. There'll be an awkward final visit.

"This, what we have now, will eventually become a painful memory." I looked up from my darkening cup of tea. I realized how horrible I was being and tried to soften my words with a smile. "If we're lucky, with time, that memory will morph from painful to wonderful." I slid my hand out from under his and lifted the tea to my lips. It was too hot, too bitter. I set the cup back down with a clatter, and some of the reddish liquid sloshed over into the saucer. A drop flew up and scalded my thumb.

Walt stared at me for a very long time. He ate one of the scones, sipped his tea. "You're probably right, Ricky. And you're absolutely right if you believe that's what'll happen. I believe wholeheartedly in the notion that our thoughts shape our reality." He took another sip of tea. "So if you think we'll end up as you just described, we will." He nodded. "Life has a funny way of giving us exactly what we expect from it.

"But for me, I like to believe that, yeah, we'll call and write. I hope you'll come up to Boston and see me before it gets cold. I hope that visit will be so special that we will immediately have to make the time and the funds available for a second visit. Then a third. And so on and so forth until we at last are busy trying to figure out a more permanent way of being together." He cocked his head. "What's the harm in believing that? We can think your way or my way, but the future will play out as it will. So why not believe that the positive might happen? Why not choose hope over despair?"

He grabbed my hand again and squeezed it. I looked up to see tears standing in his eyes. "Why not believe that love can last? And then do everything we can to make it happen."

I think that normally I would have been cheered, roused by his heartfelt speech. But this damn fatigue was only deepening, despite the doses of optimism and caffeine. I couldn't meet his hope with despair, so I forced myself to smile, even though my gut was beginning to ache. "I'm sorry to be such a downer. It's the pragmatist— no, the cynic in me. I've been unlucky in love more times than you know. My default setting is to go for another heartbreak, because that's how it always ends up for me." My smile softened, turning sad. "You're right. Maybe we can make something of this if we have hope. If we're committed. I'll come see you. I'll look into it as soon as I get home, okay?"

Walt's smile nearly broke my heart. It was full of so much joy and relief. "Really?"

"Yes, Walt, really." I squeezed his hand.

Finally, I realized that my fatigue was more than exhaustion. I worried that I was getting sick. Perfect.

I got to my feet, as surprised as Walt was by my move. But I needed to get out of there, get back to the flat and a bed. "Forgive me, but I don't feel so good."

Walt stood.

I motioned him back down. "Stay. Have your tea and scones, maybe get yourself some dinner." Just saying the words made my stomach churn.

Warily, he sat back down. "Are you okay?"

"I don't think so, but it's not to do with you." I wanted to smile, but it no longer seemed possible. As much as I wanted to deny it, I realized I was getting ill. "I just need to get back, lie down. I'm sure it'll pass after a little rest."

I didn't want to kiss him, both from not wanting to give him whatever it was I'd contracted, but also because I still had a fear of how others would react to a public display of affection between two men.

"Stay. I'll be in touch, okay?"

He nodded, looking glum. I'm sure he believed I wouldn't.

I hurried from the diner. I couldn't wait to get home. And by home, I meant the good old US of A.

Chapter Twelve

I woke early from troubled sleep. I'd tossed and turned, sweating, throughout the night. When I did manage a few minutes of sleep, I was tortured by the same dream. I was walking alone in Lincoln Park, back in Chicago. I went into one of the tunnels that run beneath Lake Shore Drive. Once under, in the light of the opening ahead, all I could see was a lone male figure. I tried and tried to get to this figure, but the more I walked, the more I ran, the more elusive the figure became. It was as though I was running in place. As much as I moved, the distance between me and the silhouette never closed.

I was still alone in the double bed when the sunlight streamed into the room. Boutros had told me the night before, "You look like hell, my darling. I know you're not used to hearing that, but it's true. I do *not* want what you're having." Even sick, I was surprised Boutros would make a reference to *When Harry Met Sally*, if that was indeed what he was doing. "I'll sleep on the couch again." He stretched and yawned. "It's actually quite comfortable. And I have the TV and VCR. I'll just pop in *Taxi zum Klo*, have a wank, and drift off into heavenly sleep." *Taxi zum Klo*, or *Taxi to the Loo*, was a 1980s German film on VHS Trevor had lying around. It was about a sex addict elementary school teacher, and it contained some very graphic sex scenes, although in its day it had *not* been considered pornography.

Boutros had stared at me after making the crack about masturbating. If he was expecting me to laugh, he was sorely mistaken.

"Thank you" was the best I could muster. I'd turned and headed toward the bedroom. My hopes of getting into bed and pulling the covers over my head were at last about to come true.

Boutros halted me in my tracks by putting a gentle hand on my shoulder. I turned and was surprised to see the concern in his brown eyes. "Are you okay?"

I shrugged. "Just a little off. Probably need a good night's sleep. I think it's all catching up with me."

"Okay, then. Our flight isn't super early. But if you're not up by nine, I'll knock."

*

Now I lay there with the sun streaming in. I should have been cheered by the golden rays. Today was the day I would go home. Despite leaving Walt behind, I was eager to get back to my own little apartment in Rogers Park, my cat, AJ, and even my job as a catalog copywriter for an office-products company. The break had been wonderful, mind-expanding even, but home was home.

And yet I felt almost too weak to get out of bed. My joints ached, and the fatigue was like a heavy, soaked blanket pressing me down.

As any sexually active gay man would back in the midnineties, I worried that this was my initial warning that my body had been infected with the HIV virus. In spite of my harlotish ways, I'd always been a stickler for condom use, whether I topped or bottomed.

Still, accidents happen. About a year ago, I had been at the Unicorn, the bathhouse on Halsted, and had let a

Tom Selleck lookalike fuck me in the steam room. We had an amazing time, until he pulled out a dick with tattered latex clinging to it. The tip of his bare cock glistened with come.

We'd both looked down as he grinned and said, "Looks like I fucked right through it."

To him it was funny, a little accident, but I'd been horrified, certain my next test would turn up positive. But it didn't. And neither did the one I had right before embarking on this very trip.

Still, there were things like windows when the virus wouldn't show up on a test. There was a margin of error. In everything.

*

I sat up, wanting nothing more than to flop back down. But a very long flight lay ahead of me, first to New York City and then on to Chicago. The day would be brutal, and I knew I only had a few hours before Boutros and I would head for Heathrow.

I told myself that getting out of bed, breathing some fresh air, and having a bite to eat would make me feel better, despite my gut arguing audibly to the contrary. My only rationale for this notion was that it had worked in the past.

Despite my desire to remain in bed until the very last minute, I forced myself to get up and find a pair of jeans and a T-shirt in the clothes scattered on the bedroom floor. I pulled these on, along with my Nikes, and hobbled to the bathroom. On the way there, I could hear Boutros snoring in the living room, or the lounge as they liked to call it over here.

In the bathroom, I bent over the sink to splash some water on my face and to dampen my wild hair. When I rose and looked in the mirror, I noticed the whites of my eyes had a sickly, yellowish tinge. I peered closer at myself in the mirror, asking my reflection, "What the hell?"

Mystified, I brushed my teeth and headed for the front door.

*

Outside, I knew I should have felt better. It was one of those mornings when the world felt newly washed, clean. Even in a metropolis like London, the breezes were fresh, sweet.

But I felt used up, like trash.

I wandered through a small street that closed to traffic in the morning to allow stalls to hawk their wares—cheap jewelry, produce, and baked goods mostly. Sugar was what I concentrated on. I bought myself a treat that would normally thrill me—a big roll glazed with melted sugar. A few days ago, this pastry would have had my mouth watering. Now, as I watched the sixtysomething white-haired lady put it in a bag for me, it might as well have been a turd.

I stopped in at a Pret a Manger to get something to wash it down with. I didn't think my stomach could handle the acid in coffee, tea, or orange juice, so I bought myself something called an orange squash.

Breakfast in hand, I headed for the park where I'd met up with Walt the night before.

Since it was so early, the park was nearly empty. For company, there was an old man sitting on a bench, reading an Agatha Christie mystery, and a young woman in jogging clothes walking briskly with a Boston terrier in a red harness.

I crossed the grass and sat down on a bench. I opened the bottle of squash and drank some of it. Encouraged, I opened the wax-paper bag containing my pastry and peered into it. The sugar-glazed treat still looked unappetizing. My stomach heaved.

I took it out, anyway, trying to be a sport, trying to cling to the belief that a little food would actually settle my stomach. I nibbled a small bite but could barely swallow it. I feared I'd throw it right back up, but I closed my eyes, willing my tummy to still. I breathed in a few slow, deep breaths.

It worked, although I still felt lousy. I managed to drink the squash, but there was no way I would risk eating the pastry. I ended up feeding it to the pigeons. Imagine their delight!

*

The airport was another ordeal. Somehow, I had been bumped from our flight and put on standby. Bad enough I was really ill, but the terror of having to navigate my way home alone was more daunting.

Boutros, God bless him, offered to stay with me so that we could fly together if I couldn't get on our original flight.

I waited and waited to learn if I was going to be onboard.

At last, the announcement came that I would be able to fly with Boutros to New York. The only thing was, the terminal we were to fly out of was switched at the last minute.

My last memory of England: dashing through the huge puzzle that is Heathrow International Airport with only minutes to spare, covered in a thin glaze of sweat and fearing I would not only not make the plane but would throw up in the process of getting there.

Fate was on my side. I made it and even managed to keep the meager contents of my stomach where they belonged.

I couldn't wait to get home.

Chapter Thirteen

Present Day

Kind reader, I hope you'll be gratified and relieved to know I made it home in one sad piece from England that long, tortuous day. Diseased, but alive.

The flight to New York from Heathrow was not without incident, the principal one being a huge blowout between Boutros and a flight attendant over a vegetarian meal. Vegetarian or not, *any* food selection wasn't an option for me. I wanted to die.

To make matters even more delightful, I was picked at random for a luggage search. Or maybe not so random—I was a sickly yellow by the time I got to New York, and perhaps that, combined with my irritated demeanor and scruffy beard, marked me as some sort of malcontent or drug abuser. Terrorists were pretty much unheard of back in '95.

Once again, I found myself late for boarding and running for my flight to Chicago too. It was my day to be winded and on the verge of vomiting.

Once I got home, the universe, in its magnanimous wisdom, had more horrors in store.

My illness climbed new heights of agony. I found I could barely get out of bed the rest of the Friday after I returned. On Saturday, I planned more of the same, bedrest and maybe a "spot of tea," hoping my friend Mary, who'd taken care of my cat, wouldn't mind doing the feline boarding thing for a couple more days, even though I didn't have the strength to ask her. I knew my beloved, fat black-and-white cat was safe with her in her Lake Michigan–adjacent condo in Evanston.

I was wrong. The phone rang early on Saturday morning, and Mary, who knew I'd gotten back the day before, barked into the phone, "Come and get your cat" and hung up.

Okay, maybe I should have called.

I managed to force myself out of bed, onto the L, and up to Evanston. AJ was thrilled to come home, and despite my sickness, I found myself happy to have the little guy around. He always sensed when I was ill, and once back at home, he installed himself next to me on my bed, a furry, purring hot-water bottle and sympathetic nurse all in one.

So what was the issue that plagued me? Those of you who are in the medical profession might have guessed, but those not in tune with yellow eyes, dark urine, aching joints, and a horrid malaise may not have surmised that I'd contracted hepatitis somewhere along the way. Whether it happened before I'd left the country or during some of my "adventures" across the pond, I found myself the proud host of a new guest, Mr. Hepatitis A, for which the only treatment, really, was resting until it chose to stop torturing me.

After a week off from work that I could ill afford, I returned to my job ten pounds lighter, lacking energy, but on the road to recovery.

And although I was still pining for Walt and shamed by an infection I had surely acquired sexually, I was also on the road to a new—and unexpected—love.

I found him in a leather bar.

*

1995

I met him at a leather bar called the Cell, just off Halsted, known for its backroom shenanigans and its strict dress code. The Cell was laid out in a three-room format. As one progressed through the three rooms, one shed inhibitions.

The first room was a regular bar, its interior echoing taverns, both gay and straight, all over the city. It contained a long wooden bar with black leatherette stools. The mirrored wall behind it reflected a fantasy land of bottles containing every color and liquor imaginable. Oblivion in rainbow shades.

The room had a worn wooden floor and TV monitors mounted high above the bar. There was a pool table in the big space at the back, and behind the pool table, a small store, set up to look like a cell, sold a few pieces of leather fetish wear, lube, poppers, and sex toys.

You could smoke back then in bars, so everything in the room wore a gauzy haze, outlines blurred in blue-gray.

The difference between the Cell and straight bars, though, was immediately apparent if you were not dressed properly to come inside. Come inside? A Freudian slip if ever one were writ. Anyway, the primary difference between the Cell and other (nonleather) establishments was that its doorman was responsible for checking IDs, *as well as* attire. No gym shoes. No cologne. No khakis. No shorts. You were permitted entry if you had on at least one (but preferably more) of the following black leather accouterments: chaps, harness, bar vest, collar, armband, or cap, usually a brimmed biker hat. You might also gain entry if you wore something made of latex or rubber. On your feet, you needed something like biker or combat boots. The doorman didn't give a damn how expensive your Nikes were!

Secondly, the TV monitors were not tuned to sports as they would be in one of the straight bars a stone's throw away, over by Wrigley Field. Nor were they broadcasting classic show-tune movie excerpts, as they would have been at the nearby Sidetrack. Dance videos? Go to Roscoe's. No, even in the front room of the Cell, you were immediately thrust (Freudian slip again? Seriously?) into the world of hard-core pornography. At any given moment, you might walk in and be treated to seeing a guy being gangbanged in a sling, or someone being fisted or pissed upon.

It was not the thing a guy like me, who'd grown up with *The Wonderful World of Disney* on childhood Sunday nights, was used to. Although I must admit I would have creamed in my jeans if Tinkerbell had shown up in any of these films to bless a come shot or two with her sparkling fairy wand.

Clap if you agree.

That was just the first room of the Cell.

The second was for the dancers. And yes, Virginia, leathermen do dance, albeit without quite the same grace as their feyer counterparts at the nearby Roscoe's. Here, the beat was heavy, techno, bone-jarringly percussive. Back then, you'd hear beats by The Prodigy, Paul Oakenfold, the Chemical Brothers, or Fatboy Slim. The room was smaller than the front bar and bright enough only to see your hand in front of your face. There was a small bar next to the glassed-in DJ booth. Dancers on the floor were mostly shirtless, with brown bottles of poppers held to their noses.

Sometimes sex broke out on the dance floor. No one seemed to mind.

Sex *always* broke out in the back room. Here, there was no bar. What you'd find was dark red walls (you'd only be privy to the color if you were here when the lights came up at the end of a night, as I'd been many times in the past) and a large leather web upon which one could offer various parts of one's anatomy to a hungry spider type. There was a St. Andrew's Cross. A sling graced the corner. And there was lots and lots of wall space against which one could lean while getting blown or cling to while getting fucked from behind.

The floor probably had enough DNA soaked into its concrete to populate an entire country. Maybe the whole world.

The pulsing techno music from the room next door would filter through but couldn't compete with the language of sighs, grunts, groans, and murmurs being spoken fluently back here.

The Cell is where I met the man who would confuse me, thrill me, appall me, and cause me to be, as the song says, "Torn Between Two Lovers."

His name was as common as he was. Tom Green. Now, if you're hoping we met in the back room, two shadows become one among a crowd of like-minded fuckers, well, darling, I'm sorry to disappoint you.

We actually met in the front bar late one night. If it's any consolation, shortly after meeting for the very first time, when Tom mistook me—bless his heart—for an adult film star whom he'd lusted after, we made our way to that very same back room. It was a way to, you know, get better acquainted. It was what one did back in the day.

But I need to tell this story my way, so let's back up to the beginning of that hot summer night so you get a handle on my frame of mind when Tom walked into my life, disrupting and delighting it.

*

That particular night when everything changed for me started, as it often did, with a phone call from Boutros. In those days, there was no texting, so we actually had to talk to one another.

"What are you doing?"

"Feeding my pussy."

"Again?"

"Get your mind out of the gutter. I'm giving AJ his supper—Meow Mix. His favorite."

"Crap."

"He loves it."

"Loving something is overrated. You love dick and eating out buttholes. Look where it's gotten *you*. Hey, how *is* that hepatitis?"

"Oh, thank you, sweetie, for showing such concern for my welfare!"

"You're welcome."

"Anyway, I'm doing okay. Back at work. White-eyed and bushy-tailed. Feeling normal again."

"That's good. Do you feel like going out for a drink tonight, then? Think your liver can handle it?"

My liver would probably be better off without an infusion of beer or spirits, and I knew it. I had a pile of laundry that needed doing. TMC was replaying one of my favorite movies, the Douglas Sirk weeper *Imitation of*

Life, and I didn't want to miss it. So naturally I said, "That sounds lovely. What time should I pick you up?" Boutros had yet to learn how to drive.

"Ten. Nothing really happens in this town until then. Even on a Thursday."

I told him I'd be by around that time.

*

Boutros and I went out to a leather bar that night, as we often did. But it was not the Cell. It was its older, and filthier, peer in Andersonville, on north Clark, the Chicago Eagle. The Eagle had all the same elements as the Cell—back room, smoke, leather guys, and porn—but they were much more egalitarian regarding who they let in.

They let in anyone. There was supposed to be a dress code, but I'd never seen it enforced. You could come dressed in your finest preppy wear, including khaki, Izod, and penny loafers, and get in—as long as you were willing to "take a knee" in the back room and, of course, buy a beverage or two.

Boutros and I, as we often did, went our separate ways after having had a beer and a smoke together. We, like so many other gay male duos who were only friends, followed the law of the jungle. Namely, to stay out of the other's way when searching for a man—whether it was for the next five minutes, for the night, or for a lifetime.

I found myself sitting alone on a built-in bench underneath a Tom of Finland poster when I was approached by a very cute bearded redhead. He was wearing tight 501s, no shirt, and a bar vest. His beard but lack of belly marked him as an otter.

"We're twins." I raised my bottle of Bud to him.

And right away, I knew he was a genius. His smile vanished as he scratched his beard. "Huh?"

I gestured to my own bar vest and Levi's, and then, to make things perfectly clear, to his. "We're wearing the same clothes."

"Oh," he uttered a grim little chuckle. I still didn't think he got my little opening gambit joke. He sat down beside me.

Normally such a lack of sense of humor (or was it lack of intelligence? Both?) would have bored me, and I would have moved on. But this guy's looks saved him. He was hot, as only little, bearded ginger boys can be. He was like a sexy leprechaun. I hoped that if I talked long enough to him, I might get a glimpse, or more, of his Lucky Charms in the back room.

He extended a hand. "Pat."

"Of course you are. I'm Ricky." We shook, and his grip was predictably close to bone crunching.

Not surprisingly, we sat quietly after the introductions. We sipped our beer and watched Al Parker stuff his balls into the ass of a willing pal in an old vintage porn on the monitor above us.

I quickly learned that Pat was not into sweet talk. He subtly moved closer so that our shoulders touched. I experienced a frisson of heat and electricity at the sensation of our sweaty bare skin uniting. He laid a hand upon my thigh.

Oh, this is going right where I want it to, I thought as his hand inched upward.

But then, without warning, he reached up, grabbed my chin roughly, and turned my face toward his. He kissed me hard, jamming his tongue down my throat. I nearly gagged. Now I had the impression he was graceless as well as clueless. And maybe, just maybe, psychotic. I understand there are those who like a little bit of rough (I'm not one of them—save for maybe a brotherly smack on the ass in the heat of passion, a sort of giddy-up kind of blow), but I would think that even those who do enjoy the rough stuff look for at least some sign of welcome.

I pushed him away—roughly—worried that he might like it. I was about to tell him to slow down a bit. A little rough was okay, but let's ease into it, okay?

But I didn't get the chance because, smiling his charming and disarming smile, he next lightly slapped my face.

My mouth dropped open. It didn't hurt. But, really? I need, I don't know what, but something more before a guy feels free to slap my face.

And then he did it again, harder.

That time stung. I imagined a welt rising up on my cheek. The heat was there.

I yanked farther away. "What's wrong with you?"

He grinned—so devilishly that I could almost forgive him. Almost.

"I thought you wanted it."

I shook my head and scooted down the bench, placing almost a foot of distance between us. "I don't know what gave you that idea." I didn't know which was worse, the actual slap, or someone thinking I'd wanted to be physically assaulted in a bar.

And as suddenly as he'd arrived, he got up and left me sitting alone with my beer.

I watched him head into the back room, where I was sadly certain he'd find someone receptive to his charms.

I looked around for Boutros.

There he was—heading into one of the men's rooms, pulling a big, hairy dark-haired lad by a leash. I followed their progress until the door closed behind them. It didn't take much imagination to figure out what would go on behind that door.

God only knew how long they'd be inside.

Another law of the jungle was that one could exit the bar, leaving the other behind at any point, if it was advantageous.

Right now, it was advantageous for me. My cheek still stung. I needed some air. Even though the bar was only about half full (or half empty), I felt claustrophobic, as though the black-painted walls were closing in.

Once I got outside on Clark, I felt better. Freer. Despite the heat, humidity, and the smell of exhaust hanging in the air—urban miasma—there was a sense of release. It was as though the evening had finally opened itself up. Anything could happen.

I thought for a moment of Boutros. He'd wonder where I'd gone, of course, but not for long. Soon he'd find himself another playmate, maybe even the slap-happy redhead. I smiled as I thought how Boutros would annihilate him, probably verbally, but maybe even physically—Boutros was a lot tougher than he appeared—if he dared smack Boutros's face.

I snorted. Now that was a funny notion.

I took in a deep lungful of bus fumes as the number 22 roared by and contemplated my options. Next door to the Eagle was the oh-so-convenient Man's Country, a multistoried bathhouse where one could find just about anything one desired, as long as those desires fell into the drug or sex category. I had a membership. But I'd just gotten over hepatitis A, and I didn't fancy catching something else tonight. When you had sex with someone at Man's Country, you had sex with everyone else they'd had sex with, and from personal experience, I knew that could be a lot of men! No, maybe another time, when my desire outweighed my common sense, which was a fairly frequent occurrence, I'm sorry to admit.

I looked the other way and thought about the little side road running along Saint Boniface Cemetery. Guys who hadn't found what they wanted at the Eagle or Man's Country often loitered there late at night in a public place, hoping for one last chance.

Why, just last fall, I'd had quite a memorable time there when I'd had my one and only sexual encounter with a ghost.

Yes, you read that right. I drifted back...

The air that September night was hot, so humid you could almost touch it. Inside the Eagle, it had been just as bad...or worse. In spite of the crowds, no one met my exacting standards, and so, plied with equal amounts of alcohol and despair, I emerged into the torpid night lit by a big tangerine moon.

I wandered over to the little side street that ran parallel to the walled northern border of Saint Boniface Cemetery. There were only a few houses, all of them dark. And the street was a dead end. I stood around, thinking nothing much would happen. I smoked a cigarette, making an agreement with myself that when it was burned down almost to the filter, I would head home. I was almost ready to make that very trip—the rumble of the L a few blocks over reminded me to get on board—when a man approached. Even in the dim light, I liked what I saw: tall, husky, dark hair flowing messily out of a Kangol cap, and eyes so mesmerizing that, for a second, I could see nothing else.

We didn't say much. Isn't it strange how gay men have elevated eye contact to a language all its own? Before long, near the wall of the cemetery, corporeal fires got ignited, and the two of us sought a place that would offer more privacy. My new friend led me to a rust-eaten pickup. I asked if it was his. He simply smiled and opened the door. He scurried inside, and I didn't hesitate to join him. Kisses resumed and went from lips to nether regions in only a minute or two.

The sweltering air, the eerie light, the thrill of getting caught, and a hot man all conspired to create a night of romance I won't ever forget. I remember the climax of our union found us this way—the truck passenger door open, my new friend prone, naked, across the front seat with his calves resting on my shoulders while I fucked him ruthlessly, my T-shirt on the ground and my camo pants around my ankles.

There were at least two full moons that night.

After it was over, and after the two of us scrambled to get dressed, we went our separate ways, he heading off in the direction of the cemetery. As soon as I started to make my way to the L, I stopped and turned around. He might also be headed for the L. It would be nice to have a repeat encounter—if not tonight, then soon. In the meantime, perhaps, we could accompany each other on the several-blocks-long walk and get better acquainted. The kindness in his dark brown eyes stuck with me, along with his quiet demeanor. Who knew, I wondered, maybe something could come of this.

But he was gone.

I searched up and down the dead-end street we'd been on and even cast a gaze along some of the side streets. He'd disappeared too quickly! There was nowhere for him to go, really, but up the dead-end street, and there wasn't time enough for him to traverse its short course. He had vanished—as unlikely or impossible at it might have seemed.

I stared at the cemetery walls as I walked away, wondering if he had emerged not from the same bar as I had, but from St. Boniface's slumbering confines, driven by needs he was supposed to have left long behind. Did we never learn to behave? I smiled at the thought, but shivered as the temperature of the night seemed to plunge downward...

I shivered now, too, at the memory. Nah, I thought, maybe I'll skip that little side street.

I wanted someone alive.

Just as it had reminded me of its existence that night last fall, I heard the rumble of the L to the east. I picked up my pace and started heading south, toward where I'd left my car.

*

At close to midnight on a Thursday night, the Cell was hopping when I walked in. The front bar was crowded with leather guys, and I was glad I'd opted to wear what I did that night. My bare chest was glazed—fetchingly, I hoped—with a light sheen of sweat. Typical for Chicago, the closest parking I could find was at least six blocks away and I'd had to hoof it from there.

After showing the doorman my ID, I looked up and grinned. Several heads had swiveled around to check me out, and some were already smiling, come-hither looks in their naughty eyes. Part of me wanted to glide through the crowd and head straight for the back room. It had been a long night, and I was starting to feel a bit of fatigue, especially after my urban hike in what had to be ninety degrees and 100 percent humidity.

I'd walked into that back room many a night, lowered my drawers, gotten a blow job from a stranger, and headed home, relieved of my burden. It wasn't exactly pretty, but it was utilitarian, right?

As I made my way through the crowd, making eye contact here and veering away from an inappropriate grope there, I was beginning to think, to hell with getting a beer—why not just act on my libido's imperative.

"It wouldn't be the first time, darling," I could hear Boutros saying in my head. "Nor the last."

"You look just like Butch Andros," someone said as I hurried by him.

Someone grabbed my back pocket, halting me in my tracks. "Hey, handsome, I'm talking to you."

What? I thought. *Another rough-trade purveyor?* I turned to glare at the person who'd accosted me and was greeted with one of the sweetest faces I'd ever seen. My outrage vanished like that ghost I told you about earlier.

I quickly rearranged my features into a questioning smile (shifting from the "What the fuck?" expression I'd had on a second before). "What did you say?"

The guy was adorable, but in a burly truck driver sort of way. As it seemed every other man in the world was, he too wore a leather bar vest and faded jeans. The bar vest exposed a very hairy chest, the fur so thick you could barely see his nipples (I would later find out he had three of them, just like Mark Wahlberg). He wore a thick studded armband around his right bicep, which was alluringly large, defined, and decorated with a Celtic circle tattoo—and which also indicated he leaned toward bottom, which was A-OK with me, at least at the moment. His whole body, all six foot two of it, I'd guessed (correctly), had about it a kind of coiled sensuality, from his mahogany and thickly curled hair, close-cropped, down to his scuffed and stained construction-worker boots.

But it was his face that really drew me. Sure, it was handsome—nice smile, incredible topaz eyes, a thick little goatee surrounding full lips—but what really hit me was the sweetness there. It was as though he expected the world to return the good he saw in it, the joy he found in other people. Now, you might ask, how could you know, in a single moment, how he felt about the world and how he was inclined toward it? To which I would answer, I don't know, but it was simply *there*. And it made me feel good, happy.

I wanted to know him better, not only sexually (that was standard operating procedure for me in my thirties, and you know it was for *you* too—come on, admit it!), but as a person.

"I said you look just like my favorite porn star, Butch Andros. He was in a bunch of old Falcon movies back in the day. Hot, hot, hot." He grinned, revealing a small gap is his front teeth that ratcheted my lust up another notch.

I looked down shyly at the floor and then back up at him. I leaned in close and said in a soft, but growlingly deep voice, "I *am* Butch Andros. Don't tell anyone, okay?"

He sat back and stiffened a little, stunned. His jaw dropped. "Really?" he asked, with a kind of childlike wonder. A blush rose to his cheeks.

I had been all set to continue the story with something about how I was going incognito tonight and that my real name was Elmer Goldstein, but when I saw that he actually believed me and didn't realize I was kidding, I quickly decided not to be cruel.

I waved his "really?" away with a hand. "No, not really. But I'm flattered that you thought so." Although I didn't know who Butch Andros was, I figured if he was a porn star in the late seventies/early eighties, he was probably pretty hot in a Tom of Finland *and* Tom Selleck sort of way.

His smile wavered, and I could tell he was both a little disappointed but maybe also (at least I hoped) relieved I wasn't, in fact, his favorite adult star. I would imagine that certain expectations would come along with successfully hooking up with a porn star. But to date I had no real-life experience with such expectations, so I was just guessing.

He swiveled on his bar stool and motioned the bartender over with a smile. They seemed to be acquainted.

He swiveled back to me. "What are you havin', handsome?"

"Oh, I can get it."

"Get outta here. I'm buyin'."

"A Bud Lite, I guess. Thank you."

He ordered the beer for me and another Jack and Coke for himself.

Once we were settled in with our drinks, me leaning toward him because there were no other empty bar stools going wanting, we exchanged names and talked briefly about the heat outside.

Which led Tom Green to motion toward the back with a little nod of his head. "I hear it's cooler in the back." Light twinkled in his eyes, and his grin was that of a little boy with a squirt gun in his hand.

"Oh? I've never been back there."

"Really?" he gasped.

I could see I wouldn't be kidding around a lot with Tom. "No, no. I've been back there." My mind honestly added *a lot* while my lips added, "A few times."

He touched my chest. "You wanna head back there for a bit? Get to know each other a little better?"

I considered—very, very briefly—saying, "Isn't that what we're doing?" but realized he might not understand I was teasing, so I just said, "Okay."

We made our way through the room with the dancers gyrating and sniffing poppers, their shirtless torsos glistening with sweat even in the dim light. I thought of choreographed mating rituals. The Prodigy's "Break & Enter" was playing, revving up my pulse rate.

We passed through the heavy black vinyl drape that separated the dance floor from the back room. Even though there was very little division between the two rooms, there was a marked difference as soon as that curtain closed. It may have been my imagination, but back here, in the deep shadows, it seemed quieter, even though that wasn't really possible. Yet there was an immediate shift from *hearing* the music to *feeling* its techno beat in my bones and gut.

Maybe the sound had a different aspect because it was *quiet* back here in terms of talking. Guys didn't come back here to chat. All that was audible were soft sighs and whispers, maybe a groan, muffled. There was no laughter—this was serious business.

Tom grabbed my hand and held it while our eyes adjusted. As mine did, I could see, over in the corner, a guy bent over, his hands on his knees. His white T-shirt glowed; it was pushed up around his neck, his pants lost in the shadows around his ankles. A big bearish type, naked save for a baseball cap, fucked him rapidly and really, really hard from behind. From the guy's excited little grunt with each thrust, I don't think he was in pain. A couple other guys loitered around the lovers, watching and perhaps waiting for their turn.

Several guys leaned against the black cinder block, flies open, while others kneeled before them, sucking.

It was like a scene from a Fellini movie.

I immediately got hard.

So did Tom, I assume. He pulled me over to a vacant area along the wall and maneuvered me so I was leaning against it. He dropped to his knees, undid his jeans, and pulled out his dick. I watched as he groped in his front pocket—he eventually produced a little brown bottle of poppers and took a big hit. Without looking at me, he stretched his arm with the bottle up so I could take it.

I took it and breathed in a lungful of butyl nitrite. As the drug hit me, causing my heartbeat to intensify to the beat of a jackhammer and beads of sweat to break out on my forehead, I could feel Tom expertly undoing the buttons on my fly. The hit had made me hungry for his mouth on my cock—desperate, really.

I didn't have to wait long. As soon as he had my dick out, he swallowed it all the way down to the root, hungrily, like a starving man. A muffled groan issued from him, and he reached up with a hand to indicate that I should hand him back the poppers.

I did. I was still riding the wave of my first hit, the blood was roaring in my ears, and I felt transported to a world where all that existed was his mouth on my cock. It was a perfectly synchronized rhapsody of spit, tongue, lips, and mouth—never teeth. It wasn't long at all until I felt the first tremors of coming. I breathed in sharply and tapped his shoulder.

He stopped and looked up at me.

"My turn," I whispered.

I didn't really want him to stop but knew if he didn't, especially with the poppers amping up my lust, I would come in no time flat. I'm sure he wouldn't have been disappointed. His expertise and experience were all too clearly on display.

He grinned and got to his feet. We switched places. Holding down his upward-pointing cock, he directed it toward my mouth. As quickly as he did with me, I swallowed the whole thing, which made me proud. It was thick, and I wouldn't have been surprised if it was over eight inches. I could imagine many a disappointed boy seeing that cock and realizing it belonged to a bottom.

But for the moment, I was the one doing the servicing. I was loving it. He held the poppers to each of my nostrils, and I took a deep hit in each one and continued, oblivious to everything but the big dick thrusting in and out of my throat.

I was in heaven.

I was working for it—a jetting mouthful of come—when Tom gripped me under my pits to yank me to my feet.

I looked at him with wonder, breathing heavily, my dick jerking up and down, on the verge of coming without even a touch.

"Hmm?" I asked. I was dying to get back on my knees.

"We should get out of here," he whispered hotly in my ear.

"You got a place?"

"Yeah, just down the street a couple blocks. We can be there in ten minutes." He leaned in closer, pressing his damp chest against mine, grinding his cock against my own. "I really want you to fuck me, man."

I smiled. "No problem."

We buttoned up, zipped up, straightened up, and headed out. As we neared the door, I asked, "So this will be your first time, right?"

"What?"

We went through the door. I noticed the doorman's gaze on us and met his stare. His grin was playful and knowing.

I waited until Tom lit a cigarette and then went on. "You know, bringing someone home from the bar. I'm sure you've never done that before. You're a pillar of virtue, right?" I managed to keep my features neutral, didn't even smile, hoping he'd get my little sarcastic joke.

He kind of did. He guffawed, expelling a cloud of smoke. "Yeah, right."

"Well, maybe the first time tonight, eh?" I nudged him.

"I don't kiss and tell."

We started down the street. I briefly thought Mr. Tom Green was a very experienced boy and, even though I was kidding about being the first guy he was bringing home from the bar tonight, I realized that I could have been one of sort of a long line. He was a ten-minute walk away.

So much for keeping my dick clean and free of infection!

But, my oh my, I thought as I leaned back to take a look at his bubble butt, the worn denim clinging to it as it rose and fell, this is totally worth whatever risk I'm about to take.

I pointed to his cigarette. "Can you spare one of those?"

He slid one out and gave it to me. We walked to his place on Cornelia wordlessly, two men sharing, I was pretty sure, the same thoughts.

*

Tom's apartment was a tiny studio—one big room with a bed shoved up against the south wall, a kitchenette opposite with a tiny table and two chairs, and finally, a big TV and VCR on a stand on the other wall. A doorway led into what I assumed was the bathroom. The floors were parquet and scuffed. There were two windows that, if I figured right, faced out to the courtyard of the yellow-brick apartment building we were in. But any views were blocked by the vinyl mini blinds Tom had in place.

He excused himself to go into the bathroom with a pointed glance. "Need to clean up, okay?"

I nodded and plopped down on his bed to check out the tiny apartment. I'd bet it wasn't more than five hundred square feet.

There were a couple of posters on the wall—the usual Herb Ritts man-candy stuff in black and white. Dishes and glasses were heaped neatly into a drainer by the sink. The walls were beige.

The place was kind of soulless, and I felt a little sad for Tom in between the currents of lust coursing through me. The apartment looked like no one had lived here and everyone had lived here. These in-need-of-paint walls had seen many a lonely gay man, I thought, throughout the years. I knew gay because we were in Boystown, with close proximity to all the gay bars. I knew men because the girls tended to congregate farther north, up on Broadway and even farther up in the Andersonville 'hood.

I noticed there were no books, and that was a little disappointing. Maybe even surpassing my love of men was my love of books. I'd read all my life—and truly was never *not* reading a book. In my many, many moves around the city to various apartments, the biggest burden was always the heavy load of boxes and boxes of books. Mysteries, thrillers, true crime, horror, biographies— from classics to utter trash, I was as indiscriminate and insatiable about books as I was about men.

The fact that the only reading material in the place was an old copy of *Entertainment Weekly* on the kitchen counter didn't bode well for this encounter going much further than a one-nighter.

And that was okay. I wasn't coming here for tea and biscuits and a nice chat about the latest Nora Roberts. We were here to fuck, and Mr. Green's reading habits really couldn't get in the way of that.

But a future? Even a date? Well, who knew?

I smelled the acrid burn of a lit match. Tom flushed.

I struggled out of my clothes in record time and lay back fetchingly on the bed, my erection pointing at the cheap cut-glass light fixture on the popcorn ceiling.

It was showtime.

*

When we were done, we lay in each other's arms atop sheets drenched in sweat. Our bodies were slick as otters. The room reeked of perspiration and come.

I marveled, "It's a wonder we're not husks."

Tom snuggled into my neck. "What do you mean?"

"Dried out, not an ounce of water left in us." I ran my forefinger along my chest. I held it up for Tom to see. A single drop dangled from my fingertip.

He lifted his head to lick it off. "Salty," he said.

We'd spent the past two hours fucking. Those poppers had come in handy because we went through three rounds. It was all me as top, but I hoped to one day turn the tables, or as they said in the sex ads, "flip fuck." I wasn't confident it would ever happen. I don't think I'd ever been with a man who loved bottoming as much as Tom.

My dick inside him seemed to take him to a place outside himself. His eyes glazed over. His toes curled. His mouth hung partially open in a kind of ecstatic joy (seriously...I'm not saying I was *that* good, just that he loved being penetrated so much). His cries, moans, whispers, and exhortations were out of the realm of mere language. What he was experiencing, I think, could never be expressed in words. Words were too meager, too crude.

He shot every time, onto his belly or onto the sheets, depending on position, without ever touching himself.

After we were done, he went into the bathroom and came back with a warm, damp towel to clean me up. There was a kind of adoration in his eyes as he stroked my belly and thighs with the towel, and a flicker of a smile playing across his features, rarely breaking contact with my eyes. Maybe the adoration I saw in his expression was my own emotion reflected back at me.

And now here we lay, a little breathless, a lot damp, sated. I haven't made any secret out of the fact that, back then, I got around. If I showed everything that had been stuck into me, I would have looked like a goddamn porcupine!

Tonight, there was something different. I felt safe here in this tiny studio apartment. I felt warm snuggled next to this big, furry man whose eyes reminded me of dark gems. Usually, after the roller coaster of lust and sex were over, I wanted to go home. I seldom even liked to stay with a one-night stand for the whole night. After the climax, or climaxes in this case, the first place my attention went was to locate my clothes on the floor, followed quickly by thoughts of how to get the hell out. "I have to get up early" usually sufficed.

"I don't think you told me what you do for a living." Wouldn't it be a scream if he said he was a librarian?

"I drive a forklift at a printing company on the South Side."

That was *so* hot. I didn't think it possible, but my dick perked up, lifting its head and sniffing around, as if asking, "Is there any more of that?"

"Really?" I had fantasized about having my own blue-collar man, but it never seemed to work out that I'd find one. Most of the boys I met in the bars and, when I was really hard up, on the phone-sex lines all seemed to be white-collar types—copywriters like me, or editors or accountants or in sales.

"Yeah." He met my gaze, and I read on his face that he was a little abashed, maybe even embarrassed. "What do you do? I bet it's something great. You seem really smart."

How he figured I was smart was beyond me, since most of our communication to this point had been nonverbal. "Ah, not much. I work for an office-products company downtown. I write copy for their catalogs."

"Copy? What's that?"

I paused. "Um, it's the descriptions of stuff for sale in the catalog, like staplers, file cabinets, and fax machines." I mock shivered. "Exciting stuff." I didn't mention that my gift for writing had been channeled into catalog copy. I couldn't allow myself to admit that when I graduated from college with my English degree I'd dreamed of being the next Stephen King. Years of rejection letters can do a lot to crush a dream.

"More exciting than what I do. But it's not a bad job. Good pay and decent benefits. They give us all a turkey at Thanksgiving and take us out for a big pizza party at Christmas—at Home Run Inn. I work with a bunch of nice folks too. I actually like it."

I bet the people he worked with adored this sweet and simple man. Tom seemed clueless to the fact that I got off on the fact that he was a salt-of-the-earth kind of guy, one who worked with his hands.

"You wear a uniform?" I was secretly hoping. Does this mean I fetishize the working class? No contest, your honor.

"Yeah," he said with a sigh. "And, in case you're wondering, I have my name stitched on the chest of it." He grinned a little devilishly, and I realized he probably wasn't as clueless about his blue-collar charm as I'd previously thought. "I wear steel-toed boots too."

I rolled over so that our entire bodies were locked together. "Hot. Would you wear it for me sometime?"

He seemed puzzled that I would ask this, but he said, "Yeah, sure."

And just like that, I found myself ready for round four.

I rolled Tom over on his side, facing away. I wondered if my dick would have any skin left on it come morning.

I pushed into him. Skin regenerates, right?

Chapter Fourteen

When I got home the next morning, the phone was ringing. It was super early. I'd left Tom as dawn was filling his apartment with grayish light, giving form and definition to his thrift-store furniture. He had to be at work much earlier than I did, and I was amazed at how close he cut it, given that he had to drive down to the South Side. But he hit snooze half a dozen times before he finally rolled out of bed with a groan. He rubbed his eyes and reached for his cigarettes.

I looked over at the alarm clock on the plastic cube by the bed. "I thought you had to be in by seven o'clock."

"I do." Tom was rapidly pulling on boxer briefs, socks, and his uniform. He patted down his pockets, repeating a little mantra, "Wallet, keys, comb, smokes," several times before he was satisfied.

"But it's twenty till."

He smiled. "I know. I'll make it."

I shook my head, relaxing into the warm covers. "You be careful." I cocked my head. "Do you do this every day?"

"Yeah, I like to get every bit of sleep I can." He leaned over to give my crotch a little squeeze. "I really needed it this morning. You gave me quite the workout last night."

"The feeling's mutual, bud." I glanced over to the hardwood floor and the half-dozen filled condoms scattered there. I thought, good thing he doesn't have a dog. *Ugh.*

He paused a few steps away from the bed and turned around. "Ricky, so glad we met last night. Seriously, dude. You're awesome. I can't wait to see you again."

"If you don't kill me first," I quipped.

"You're strong. Really strong—a real man. Grrr. Anyway, sorry I have to rush out like this. There's Frosted Flakes and Froot Loops in the cupboard above the sink, and I think there's some milk in the fridge. Help yourself. Just make sure to lock the door on your way out, okay?"

I nodded. I still needed to get to my own place, change clothes, and get downtown to work by nine, so I knew I wouldn't have time for the sweet treats he'd offered. And I wouldn't be able to indulge my nosiness, either, alone in a strange new guy's apartment. Hey, I'm not above it! Would you be?

But there was one sweet treat I didn't want to do without. "Hey!" I called after him; he was almost to the door. "Don't think you can just leave here without a kiss goodbye."

"Oh, I'm sorry." He'd returned to give me a kiss so passionate that if it had gone on a second or two longer, we both would have been late for work, perhaps even absent from work.

And now I hoped the phone wouldn't stop ringing as I groped for my keys and then hurried to unlock my door. Just like in the movies, I dropped the keys as I rushed.

I almost tripped over AJ, who lay cunningly in front of the door. I imagined him snickering to himself as I rushed across the room to quiet the ringing phone. I promised myself, once again, to get out to Target or Best Buy over the weekend and get myself an answering machine. It seemed like everybody had one but me.

Answering the call was critical because it could either be my mom, back in Ohio, who would only call this early if there was something wrong, a family emergency or the like, or Tom, missing me.

I did get to the phone in time. Turns out it was neither of my guesses. Turns out it was someone who was not calling so early at all—for his time zone.

"Ricky?"

The voice sounded familiar.

"Yeah?"

"I didn't wake you, did I? As the phone was ringing, I remembered you're an hour earlier than I am. I almost hung up but then realized that would be even more annoying."

Oh my God, it was Walt. Even though I knew that, technically, I had no reason to feel guilty, I did anyway, product of a Catholic mom as I was. A hot rush of shame burned my cheeks, as though Walt could see not only from where I'd come, but what I'd spent the night doing. His heart was broken, and I was a wanton slut.

"I was up," I said. I always said I was up—even if someone woke me out of a deep sleep. I don't know why. It seemed impolite not to. "Walt! It's good to hear your voice."

I could hear him breathe a little sigh of relief. "I'm so glad I didn't get you out of bed."

I didn't mention that I had not been in bed at all—my own, anyway. Again, the rush of shame and guilt that felt like pure, liquid heat coursed through my veins. "Nah, I was just getting ready for work."

"What is it you do again?"

I told him, glancing over at the marble antique clock I had on an old walnut secretary near the front door. My mom had given it to me for my birthday a couple of years ago. I couldn't talk long. Even if I jumped into the shower this very moment, I would be cutting it close, especially with the vagaries of the Chicago Transportation Authority.

Ah, I'd just have to be a little late today. My boss was a fifty-something queen, bitter, cutting, and, I suspected, a little in love with me. I could trade on that this morning. He'd forgive me, especially if I wore my most faded and tightest Levi's 501s with my cowboy boots. Besides, I needed to give a little time to Walt to assuage my guilt.

I told myself I had nothing to feel guilty about. Walt and I had had an amazing time together. And I saw potential for us, if we could manage, unlike so many others, to beat the long-distance romance thing. But we were hardly married, or even engaged. Hell, we weren't even going steady.

Even though my head told me all these things, my heart wasn't listening.

"Walt, it's so good to hear your voice," I repeated. "I've been thinking about you." Hey, it was true. I had! "I miss you," I added.

"I feel the same. Which is why I'm calling."

"Oh?" I wondered if he was about to tell me he'd booked a flight to Chicago. Now wouldn't it be interesting, perhaps even farcical, to have Walt *and* Tom together in the same city? I imagined briefly being out on a date with both of them, perhaps in a restaurant with two rooms where I could keep them separate. I'd be madly dashing between the two, pretending I only had eyes for one.

And then I would call Walt Tom or Tom Walt.

I giggled. This was straight out of a situation comedy. Hadn't I seen it, in fact, as a very little boy on *The Patty Duke Show*?

"What's funny?" Walt asked, yanking me out of my reverie.

"Oh, nothing. Just a thought. You were telling me why you were calling."

"Yeah. I was hoping I could interest you in coming out east for a visit. As if I weren't enough of an incentive—" Walt paused to chuckle. "—I can sweeten the pot with this: my friend, Lawrence, never Larry, who's a pretty successful fashion designer, has a gorgeous home up in New Hampshire. His house sits on land that used to be a big hippie commune." Walt laughed again. "And now he owns it, and it goes against everything the hippies stood for back in the day. Which is to say, the house is gorgeous, a capitalist dream. Beautiful pool, mountain views, rustic elegance in around five thousand square feet. The best part is—it can be our romantic hideaway for Labor Day weekend. Lawrence will be in Milan then, and who knows where after that. But he's offered me the use of the house, and I immediately thought of you—and of us. Say you'll come."

Labor Day was only a few weeks away. Without warning or even conscious provocation, an image flashed into my mind. Tom, lying on his side, asleep next to me. There was something childlike and innocent about his slumber, in contrast the big-beast sexiness of him.

Did I really want to leave him behind? Did I really want to leave *his* behind?

Besides, I didn't even know if I could afford a plane ticket this close to the holiday weekend. I was sure fares would be steep. In England, I'd made the mistake of treating pounds like dollars, and now, as the credit card statements were rolling in, I saw what an expensive assumption that had been.

"Ever made love on a pool float?"

"Ever fallen asleep looking up through a skylight at a New England country sky?"

"Ever woke to a man making you fresh ground coffee in a French press? And an omelet with herbs from a garden and homegrown tomatoes and spinach?"

"Ever drifted off with a man's arms around you and a chilly, but sweet, fresh breeze blowing in through the open window?"

I sighed. It did sound tempting. And I could charge a plane ticket. I mean, I shouldn't run up my credit card any more than I had. But hey, it wasn't maxed out. Yet. And when did opportunities like this come my way?

"You'd fly into Boston, grab the T into town, and then there's an easy bus up to New Hampshire. I don't have a car, but I have a friend, Camille, who can pick you up at the station and then deliver you to me, like a pizza. And, like a pizza, I will devour you while you're still hot."

"I'm always hot. And I have a very nice pepperoni, if I may say so."

"You may, because it's true. So, what do you think, Ricky? Can I count on you? After we spend a few days up at the retreat, we can come back to Boston, and I can show you around. You've never been, right?"

"I've never been." And I'd always wanted to visit, back from the time I was accepted to Emerson College on the Charles River and my parents told me they were proud of me but the school was out of reach for them financially. My heart still ached about that one.

"Well then, come. Beyond a plane ticket, I promise you won't have to buy another thing."

"So you understand I'm just a poor boy."

He laughed. "We are not going there. I know Queen lyrics too. And 'Bohemian Rhapsody' is my favorite of theirs. I'm sure somebody loves you."

Aw, now that was sweet. I was warming more and more to this idea. It was indeed a possibility.

And I did want to see Walt again, despite all the deluxe and romantic promises. Just seeing him once more would be amazing. And maybe it would help me sort out my rapidly developing feelings for both him *and* Tom.

But then seeing Tom again would also be amazing. And he was only a few L stops away. Easier access. Cheaper.

Sexier? Oh, who knew?

"Listen, I'm gonna be late for work. Can I check into flights and get back to you?"

"Sure. I'll take that as a yes?"

"Maybe. Have a good day, Walt. I'll call you either later today or tomorrow, okay?"

"You better."

We hung up, and I thought of two roads diverging in a wood.

*

I called Walt the next night, hoping he wouldn't answer. But he did.

I'd been about to leave a message saying I'd checked into flights and they were simply beyond my very meager budget, which was true. I hadn't actually checked but had decided, as I sat writing copy for a walnut credenza, that I was chasing after a pipe dream in getting together with Walt again. I was spending money I simply didn't have. I was pursuing a love that logic told me couldn't come to be.

And then there was Tom. We'd had only one night together. I had one-night stands all the time, more than I cared to admit. But this one had been special, not only because the sex was red-hot supernova, but because there was something about Tom that was the polar opposite of Walt. He was simple and good. Not that Walt wasn't good, but he was definitely a lot more complicated, which both repelled and drew me near. Go ahead and make that moth to a flame comparison. It's apt.

But the point was that there were plenty of fish in the Chicago sea, and I had a good one, maybe, on the hook. I didn't need to travel a thousand miles for a man or even for a city as charming and historic as I'd always heard Boston was. Or a weekend retreat at a sumptuous getaway in New Hampshire where I could fall asleep with a man's arms around me, staring up at the stars.

Oh shit.

"Hey, Walt, it's me."

"I've been waiting for your call. So? Did you book a ticket?"

The refusal, the sensible and financially prudent thing to do, was right on the tip of my tongue. "Yes," I said. "I sure did."

I could hear him clapping. "You don't know how happy this makes me."

"I do know. I do, because it makes *me* ecstatic." I'll be even more ecstatic, I thought, once I get off the phone and track down a reasonably priced plane ticket to Logan International, if such a bird exists.

"We're going to have an amazing time! I can promise you that."

"I have no doubt."

"Hang on. Let me grab a piece of paper and a pen so I can jot down your flight details."

Uh-oh. I thought fast. "I'll email you the itinerary. I can't remember specifics right offhand. Plus you don't have to worry about writing anything down."

"Good thinking. I'll reply with exactly what you need to do when you get off the plane so you'll have everything you need to come to me, sweet boy."

"I can't wait."

"I can't either. Hurry, Labor Day."

Yeah. Hurry.

I once again told Walt I'd send him details, and then we hung up.

I headed toward my dining room and my computer. Time to research some flights.

Just as I was about to sit down, the phone rang again. I hopped up and dashed to it, thinking it must be Walt, telling me something he'd forgotten to mention.

"Hey there," I called cheerily into the phone.

"Hey yourself," a deep voice came back at me, one that wasn't Walt's.

I bit my lip. "So... What's up?"

Laughter. "You don't know who this is, do you?"

I was pretty sure it was Tom but not positive. I didn't want to risk it. I'd given my number out to more than a few guys. I'd be lying if I said they didn't call at all hours with all different sorts of propositions. Sometimes, late at night, they even showed up at the front door, calling up to my balcony as Marlon Brando once did to Stella.

"Of course I do. It's you. And there's no one like you, you sexy man."

"You're so full of shit. It's Tom! How are you?"

I laughed. "I knew it was you."

"Right."

"I'm good." Again with the guilt, because I'd just gotten off the phone with another man, promising to rendezvous with him in the not-too-distant future. I was beginning to wonder if I was as free-spirited as I thought I was. Maybe monogamy, long scorned, was really what I wanted. It certainly would be easier than this juggling act I found myself beginning.

"I told myself *not* to call you," Tom said.

"Oh? Why?"

"Don't you know the rule? All my buddies, both gay and straight, tell me not to call a guy the day after, you know? They say you should wait at least a day or three. Otherwise it makes you seem too eager. But what the fuck, I *am* too eager, so I called. Hope you don't mind I'm so pathetic." He laughed.

"I don't think you're pathetic. It's sweet. And I'm thrilled to hear your voice."

"Even if you didn't recognize it." Tom chuckled. "It's okay. We just met."

There was silence for a few moments, and then Tom said, kind of quietly, "I've been thinking about you all day. I mean, like, nonstop. Just to let you know, that doesn't happen with every guy I meet. In fact, I can honestly say I can't remember when it last did, if it ever did."

I realized the same had been true for me.

"So when can I see you again?" There was such hope in his voice! It lifted my spirits way, way up.

I thought, as he had, that maybe I should try not to appear too eager. After all, weren't things better if you had to work at them to get them? Didn't they always say that delaying gratification made the reward all the sweeter? So I said, "I'm not doing anything tonight."

"Perfect. I'll come by in a couple hours. You're not too far from Leona's, right? We can go to dinner." He took in a breath. "And then come back to your place for dessert. I'm in the mood for something cream filled."

"Lord, man. You're going to be the death of me."

"Hope not. I have lots of plans for you."

"Okay, sounds good. I'll be outside waiting for you in a couple of hours, okay? You get off at the Jarvis Avenue stop."

"Got it. Address?"

And I gave it to him willingly. Along with, I was afraid, a piece of my heart. Labor Day, and Walt, were already fading fast in my memory.

I was giddy with anticipation. I dropped my clothes as I headed for the bathroom.

*

One of the things I loved most about my apartment on Fargo Avenue, in the far-north neighborhood of Rogers Park, was that it was old. As in, vintage. It had a history—and the writer in me could imagine all the stories, lives, and ghosts that had passed through my living space throughout the many decades it had stood. Sometimes I thought I could feel those lives around me. One day, I thought maybe I'd write a book and call it *Apartment 202* and write a chapter for each decade, shining a spotlight on the joys and tragedies that had taken place within the walls of my apartment. Maybe it would be bestseller.

But being old also had drawbacks, though not many. Back around the turn of the century, they built these places to last. I may have had to put up with no electrical outlets in the bathroom and separate hot- and cold-water spigots, but I had a lovely, deep porcelain claw-foot tub to soak in, which I did in anticipation of Tom's arrival. I scrubbed carefully, getting into every nook and cranny because I knew *he* would get into every nook and cranny. I'd learned fast that our Tom was a thorough man.

After I dried off and dressed in a pair of camouflage cargo shorts, a black tank, and combat boots, I went out onto another part of the old, decrepit apartment I simply adored—its balcony. I sat on the wide redbrick and concrete-topped edge to look down over the street as I smoked a cigarette and watched for Tom. The balcony had been a major selling point when I'd first looked at the apartment a couple of years ago. The L train was right next door, so it wasn't the quietest spot in the universe. But it also looked out on my tree-lined street. In fact, almost directly in front of the balcony, separated only by the cracked sidewalk below, was a large maple tree. Now that it was summer, it was heavy with verdant leaves that whispered in the breeze and softened the rumble of the L a few feet away. Dead-ending at Paulina Avenue a block to the west, Fargo was pretty, lined with old brick-courtyard apartment buildings in yellow or red. They made me feel I was not only part of a real community in this sprawling metropolis, but also like I was part of a history. I often imagined the many lives that had been played out on this block. There was a quaint neighborhood feel that made me content with my home.

My heart gave a little lurch, and I smiled. There Tom was, walking up Ashland Avenue, presumably fresh off the L train that was just now rumbling into Howard Street, the North Side terminus for the Red Line.

Tom was unaware he was being watched, and I was grateful for the chance to observe him. Although I too was done up in "gay clone" attire, I bristled a bit at how flamboyantly he was dressed—in faded Daisy Dukes, construction-worker boots, and a flannel shirt that he'd cut the sleeves off of and left open almost to his navel, to better show off, I assume, the thick mat of fur there. It *was* sexy, I had to admit, but it also screamed "flaming homosexual," and in my neighborhood, with its mixture of ethnicities, gangs, and thugs, I feared for his safety.

I also feared for his common sense.

Despite being a little apprehensive about how Tom dressed, like a gay hooker fantasy straight out of Tom of Finland or, perhaps, Falcon Studios, I was charmed and a little aroused by the sight of him. Even from where I sat on my balcony, I saw a sweet wistfulness and anticipation on his face. I imagined he viewed my neighborhood in a different way than I did, focusing on the trees, the grass, the smell of Lake Michigan a few blocks over, instead of the flaws I couldn't avoid picking up on during my trek home from work every day—the gang tags, the litter (including used needles and condoms) in the gutters, the weed-choked cement of the sidewalks.

In short, I suspected, with little good reason other than intuition, that Tom was a happy fellow because the lens through which he processed the world was a rose-colored one.

And maybe he had the right idea. After all, the world was really not a place of blacks and whites or good and evil. The world just *was*. We humans, with our egos and endlessly busy minds, assigned the meanings.

It wasn't long before he approached my front door. I didn't want him to ring the buzzer. It emitted a loud and shrill mechanical bark that always sent AJ scurrying under a piece of furniture. It also was useless as a two-way communication system (press a buzzer and hear a Charlie

Brown teacher voice come out of the speaker!), which is a large part of the reason I often perched on the edge of this very balcony near the time I knew guests might arrive.

Little secret—being up here in the trees, also allowed me to rate hookups I'd met via the phone-sex lines, to see if the way they'd described themselves was accurate. If it wasn't, I could simply turn out the lights and wait until they went away. I know what you're thinking—"You're terrible, Muriel." But hey, if a man describes himself as having a swimmer's build on the phone and doesn't bother to mention he means Shelley Winters in *The Poseidon Adventure*, he deserves to be stood up.

"Hey, you!" I leaned over the balcony's edge to look down at the top of his head, thick with curly auburn hair.

He seemed a little startled and then peered up, squinting, to locate from where my voice was coming. When he saw me, his face practically glowed, breaking into a radiant smile that was one part relief and the other joy, with perhaps a little desire mixed in. Well, maybe more than a little.

"Ricky!" he cooed.

"Hang on, I'll buzz you up. Just come to the second floor."

I turned to go inside. When I opened the balcony door, AJ rushed out, and I was grateful once more he was a cat smart enough not to try a leap off the ledge. He jumped up and then sat, enjoying the dusky breeze and licking his paws while yet another L train passed behind him. He was used to their rumble and spark, a true city feline.

After remotely unlocking the vestibule door, I listened as Tom lumbered up the stairs.

I threw open the door and smiled. He bustled in, smelling of whiskey and cigarettes, and gathered me in his arms, kicking the door closed behind him as he did so. He kissed me so deeply and passionately, I forgot all about my resolution to tell him to button up his shirt before we headed out to dinner. In fact, it wasn't long before I was unbuttoning that same shirt even farther. Once I had it open, I went to work on his nipples, making him laugh, squirm, and yip. I worked my way down his body, my tongue caressing every hirsute inch.

He pulled back a little and, panting, grinned down at me.

"You sure know how to welcome a guy!" I could see from the bulge in his shorts that he was definitely not complaining. I thought it better not to mention that I had lots of practice giving out exactly this kind of welcome.

Instead, I took his hand and led him into my bedroom. We didn't say a word as our clothes floated magically into the corners of the room. I'd hoped maybe this time I'd get to see how versatile Tom could be, but he had other ideas. In no time at all, he was on his knees on the edge of my bed, and I was poised standing behind him, drilling into him as though tomorrow might never arrive.

We paused only once, to allow Tom to switch from all fours onto his back, legs in the air, while I continued to stand. I had to do a lot of the work, but this is *not* me complaining.

When we were done, we lay crosswise on the bed before the big front window that faced the street. Darkness had fallen, and there was a yellow glow from the streetlight outside. A breeze with only the tiniest hint of a chill in it blew in, drying the sweat on our bodies.

I dragged my hand across the forest growing on Tom's chest. "Are you hungry?"

"For more?" he asked, his hand whispering across my thigh.

"Well, yeah. But I meant for some, you know, sustenance."

"Oh yeah, dinner. I'd forgotten the purpose of our date."

"Well, we both know we just made the most of the *real purpose* of our date. No use kidding ourselves, but I could use something to eat. Besides you, I mean."

"Why not? I'm delicious!"

"You are!" I tweaked his nipple hard enough to make him scream. "But I need some pasta carbonara."

Tom rubbed at his nipple, his lower lip jutting out. "That hurt." And then he replaced my hand on his chest. "Do it again."

And I did. And that's not all I did again.

We didn't get to the restaurant until almost ten o'clock.

Once we were seated in the near-empty Italian joint, we ordered almost everything on the menu and drank two bottles of red wine.

We'd worked up an appetite and were feeling quite depleted.

The wine released what few inhibitions we had, and by the time we walked back to my place again, we were ready for round three, this time on the balcony.

I was surprised we didn't get the police called on us, or worse, because of all the noise we made as I fucked him and at last—sing it, Etta James!—he fucked me. Glory hallelujah, he might describe himself as a power bottom, and that might be from where he derived most of his carnal pleasure, but that boy's dick was nice—and he knew how to use it.

We went to sleep that night in each other's arms with a fan blowing on us. I couldn't remember the last time I'd slept so peacefully.

In the morning, when we were hurrying around to get ready for work, my phone began to ring.

I ignored it.

Chapter Fifteen

The weeks leading up to Labor Day weekend passed in a blur.

First, it was a really busy time for me at work—my boss expected overtime every night, and I often found myself, along with the other copywriters and graphic designers, working on Saturdays for a bit of overtime pay and Giordano's pizza. The extra money, tired as it made me, would help pay for the insanely overpriced airline ticket I'd acquired with my credit card for my trip to Boston. More about that in a minute.

Second, Tom's and my relationship had been growing like dandelions. I say that because dandelions are the mixed bag of the horticultural world. In bloom, they're kind of sweet in their simple and sunny beauty. Their leaves can also be delicious in a salad, as my Sicilian mother had taught me.

But.

Dandelions were also weeds, capable of choking off other more desirable plants and eventually turning into an unwelcome blight.

Now, I'm not saying that Tom was becoming an unwelcome blight. Quite the contrary. Our "relationship," if you could call it that, was going relatively well. If by relatively well you mean hot sex whenever and wherever we could find it. The man was insatiable, and his love for dick knew no bounds. I would have once said that of myself, but Tom put my own horn-doggery to shame. He made me look like the singing nun.

In the past few weeks, we had fucked and sucked countless times at not only my place and his place, but in the back rooms of all three leather bars, along with the "back forty" outdoor area of an iconic sleazy bar farther south on Halsted. Tom was like me in that he liked an audience—we both enjoyed putting on an occasional show, whether the show was inadvertent or purposeful. The inadvertent shows were the ones in his studio, when the headboard banging, mattress squeaking, and moaning and groaning reached such a crescendo that his downstairs neighbor, furious and sleep-deprived, would bang on the ceiling with a broomstick. Did that stop us? Quiet us down? What do you think?

We made use of friends' cars, alleyways, and the bushes of public parks.

Between Tom and work, I could hardly see straight. And simple pastimes, like TV and even eating, fell by the wayside. I lost over ten pounds in a few weeks—and these were pounds I needed, dammit! I think I lost them all in sweat.

But when we weren't making the beast with two backs, I have to admit, we were getting to know each other intimately in other ways. And Tom continued to charm me with his reliably sweet disposition and his kindness. It was a real treat to be around someone who never complained, who always saw the best in people, and who found hope in the direst of situations. He cried easily, gave away his meager earnings to homeless people, and was always there when a friend needed help moving, a shoulder to cry on, a can of chicken soup when ill—my Tom was no cook, but his heart was always in the right place—my list of his kindnesses, small and large, could make up its own separate book.

And he never, ever expected a thing in return. Tom was always about giving.

His mom was a good example of his heart. Tom took me to meet her one Sunday, the day she typically had him over for dinner. She and Tom, he'd informed me before we met, had been a "me and you against the world" unit while Tom was growing up. "My dad threw her out when he found out I wasn't his." The story went that Tom's mother, Linda, who'd plied the bartender trade all of her adult life, had found a man at the bar she worked at back in Idaho before Tom was born—a man who could take her mind off the husband who beat her and the two screaming kids he did absolutely nothing to help care for.

"She thought she was in love with this guy. Thought he was gonna ride in on a white horse and take her away from her shitty life, the husband who cheated and drank like a fish, the ungrateful kids, the roach-infested apartment they all lived in.

"Ma really loved my dad, I think. Not so much that bastard of a husband.

"But when he found out he'd knocked her up, he took a powder. Mom never saw him again, and she won't tell me who he was. Says he doesn't deserve to know what a fine son he has. She was miserable and thought about giving me up, but she soldiered on, working and taking shit from her hubby and the kids. When I was born, I guess the truth came out. Her husband got suspicious. He'd heard things, and even as a baby I looked nothing like him or my half-sibs. So he demanded a paternity test.

"And Ma and I found ourselves out on our asses. A blessing, man! We came to the South Side of Chicago to live with her ma, my grandma."

Tom had shrugged. "It hasn't been a bad life. She did her best with me. And I could be a challenge. Believe you, me!"

That last admission didn't surprise me. Tom drank, I feared, like his mother's ex-husband, even if he hadn't inherited his genetics. I'd seen him consume worrisome amounts when we went out to the bars together. It didn't surprise me when he told me the story of his DUI and his scary night in jail.

Anyway, I'm getting off track here. I wanted to tell you about Tom's sweetness as a son and how it pulled at my heartstrings.

Linda Green and her mom lived in an old brick apartment building in a neighborhood on Chicago's Near South Side known as Bridgeport, within view of the spires of All Saints-St. Anthony Catholic Church, which Tom told me Linda and her mom, Viola, attended regularly. Bridgeport was famous in Chicago for its pizza, breaded-steak sandwiches, and being the home of something like five of the city's mayors. Despite the latter distinction, it was mostly a hardscrabble working-class neighborhood, one of the most ethnically diverse in the city (along with my own Rogers Park).

Linda's building was a four-story walkup, with a little Korean-owned grocery store and a pool hall on the ground floor. Tom and I entered through a door off the small parking lot at the rear of the building.

When Linda opened the door to us, you'd think this mother and child reunion was taking place after years of not seeing each other, instead of a mere seven days. They hugged for a long time, and I was amazed to find that when they finally pulled away, clinging to the other's hands, tears stood in both their eyes.

Linda sniffed, looked at me, and smiled. She was beautiful but careworn, with a halo of bleached-blonde hair, soulful brown eyes, and cupid's bow lips that reminded me shamefully of her son. She was a tiny little thing, clad in tight jeans, a cropped pink angora sweater, and heeled boots. If it weren't for the lines around her eyes and mouth that told a tale of a hard life, I would have imagined she was at least a decade younger than the late forties I knew she was.

Her dark eyes drank me in. And then her gaze moved toward her son. "You told me he was handsome, but wow." She laughed, and I could hear the young girl she had been. She took my arm and guided me into the apartment. I could smell a roast in the oven, and it made my mouth water.

"Oh my God, that smells great."

Linda shook her head. "It's nothing. Chuck roast, potatoes, carrots, water, and an envelope of Lipton's French Onion soup mix."

The apartment reminded me of Tom in that it was neat, but economically furnished. Most of the stuff, from the early American living room suite to the laminate dinette set in the kitchen, appeared to be either decades old or secondhand. Still, the walls were a cheerful yellow. These were hung with pictures of Tom from babyhood up to what I guessed would be his senior picture from high school. It was a little like a shrine.

I better never do this guy wrong, I thought, or I'll have Mama Bear to contend with.

An older woman sat in a recliner near the front window. She got up as I moved farther in. Like her daughter, she was very thin and only a little over five feet tall. Her hair was dyed a similar auburn shade to Tom's, but was in a tight perm. She also had dark brown eyes.

"This is my mom, Viola." Linda thrust me a little toward the older woman, who held out her arms.

A little awkwardly, I hugged her. She smelled of talcum powder and cigarettes.

We stepped away, and she said in a deep, raspy voice I wasn't expecting, "It's very nice to meet you, young man. Tom has told us all about you."

"All good, I hope?"

She waved me away. "If it was all good, I'd know him for a liar." She winked. I liked her.

The afternoon was delightful and made me a little homesick for my own family back in Ohio. Tom was such a dutiful son and grandson, helping with the mashed potatoes, setting the table, making sure his mom never carried anything too heavy, and, in general, jumping in wherever he could lighten someone's load.

He and I washed the dishes at the meal's end.

And when we left, I knew I'd want to come back again. In just one visit, they'd all three made me feel as though I belonged, that I was part of the family. I could see sitting at that laminate table at Christmas or Thanksgiving.

I think that feeling led me into the beginning of falling in love with Tom. Here I was seeing a family not rich at all in material things, but very wealthy in terms of bottomless reserves of love.

Tom and I went to sleep that night in each other's arms and, for once, didn't make love.

But I felt curiously, yet completely, at home.

Chapter Sixteen

You may be wondering what the hell happened to Boutros? You might be saying, "He figured so prominently in the first part of the story, and now it seems like he's vanished, or you dumped him as a friend."

I'm embarrassed to admit the latter, the part about dumping, is more than a little bit true. Now don't get the wrong idea—I didn't feel any less affection for Boutros, and I assume he felt the same about me as he always did. Our bitter backbiting and insults were a curious kind of love, but make no mistake—they were love. No one else but he could tell me I had a face that looked like "a smacked ass" and make me feel seen and, maybe, a little bit adored.

Ours was a strange and unique relationship.

But it worked.

The truth is, I'd fallen prey to what many of us have when we begin to fall in love, or in lust, or become infatuated—whatever you want to call it. Friends often experience a little hiatus when a new love interest comes into the picture, and that's what had happened between Boutros and me. The phenomenon of ignoring one's friends when a new love appears on the scene, I believed, was a time-honored law of the jungle.

Yet I did feel guilty about not getting together with him over the past couple of weeks or so but figured he'd understand. A man *always* trumps a friend, right?

Ah, even I didn't buy that. How could I? I could have at least called him, updated him on my dilemma of meeting not one, but two men I could well be falling for. He'd call me a slut, and I'd tell him he was heartless. We'd laugh and make plans to meet up for breakfast at the Melrose, a Boystown institution known for its greasy fare, late-night hours, and its clientele, almost all of whom were gay.

As it turned out, I'd been a very bad friend indeed.

What happened was I did try to call him on the Monday after dinner with Tom and his mom. I tried before work (Boutros was a chronically early riser—it was when he got his best writing done, he said). I called again on my lunch hour and then again when I got home from work that night around six thirty.

There was never an answer, which was odd. Unlike me, Boutros did own an answering machine, and I'd left messages each time I called. The first was a breezy kind of "Hey girl, what's up?" message. But the subsequent ones got progressively more desperate and worried.

Where was he? My best friend rarely didn't pick up the phone. And even if he was out and about, he'd always return my call.

Always.

I got a chill, a premonition that things were simply not right. You may say I was worrying needlessly. After all, it was only one day and three missed calls, a trifle for almost any other adult. Hardly an excuse to file a missing person's report.

But you don't know Boutros. He may be eccentric, cut from a cloth no one else had ever seen, but as a friend, he was unfailingly reliable.

I decided I needed to drop by, just to make sure he wasn't lying naked and rotting in his apartment, smelling of decomposition and Christmas pudding.

I dressed hurriedly and headed out to make the journey over to his place. I knew it was going to take longer than I wanted, especially because I was anxious and also because patience has never been one of my virtues.

Boutros lived in a gigantic apartment overlooking the Chicago River in a very quiet, tucked-away West Side neighborhood of Chicago called Ravenswood Manor. To get to him involved taking the Red Line L down to Belmont, switching for a Brown Line train out to Francisco, the street-level stop in Boutros's quaint neighborhood. Once you got off the train, you felt as though you'd stepped back into a more idyllic, quieter era.

He'd lived there for years, holed up in his roomy two-bedroom with oak floors, a fieldstone fireplace, crown molding, and thousands and thousands of books. I suspect the books were the reason he'd never bought himself a house or a condo when he could well afford it. The prospect of moving all those books was simply too daunting.

Anyway, I arrived at the Francisco stop almost an hour after leaving my apartment. There was a delay at Belmont, and I watched in vain as two delayed westbound trains rushed by me, running express, leaving me in a breeze of longing and disappointment.

But the good old CTA did eventually deliver me to my desired location, anxious and annoyed. It was twilight, and there was a chill breeze as I hurried down the tree-lined streets to Catalpa Avenue. Boutros's two-flat apartment building was at the eastern end of the street, where it dead-ended at the river.

I looked up at the windows of Boutros's second-story flat with despair. They were all dark, and it was getting late enough, the sky various shades of lavender and darker blue, that he should have had at least a few lights on.

When I reached his door, I rang the bell, hopeful he was just napping or watching porn or conducting a séance, whatever kind of things he'd do that required no light. Nothing he might be doing would surprise me.

I rang and rang, the hope dribbling out of me like a pricked water balloon. My worry felt like needles under my skin. A growing dread was creeping up.

I sighed and was grateful that I could at least resort to desperate measures. Well aware that I could be interrupting a passionate three-way with a Polish saxophone player and an African-American truck driver, I stooped down in the darkness and lifted the potted ceramic plant to the right of his door.

He'd told me the location of the key a long time ago, and I'd filed it away for an emergency like this one.

My hands trembled a little as I attempted to fit the key to the lock. I had a bad feeling, so it took me three tries to get the door open.

Once I went inside, I dashed up the creaking stairs, hoping against hope I'd find him okay. But another part of me, the reasonable, non-Pollyanna side, worried about what I might find, so much so that I paused at the front door at the top of the stairs.

Boutros usually never locked this door, as far as I knew, so I hoped that would continue to be the case.

It wasn't.

The door was locked, and I whispered, "Shit." I pounded on the door, again and again, my heart beating faster, certain it wouldn't be opened from inside.

But it was.

Boutros stood before me. The blank stare on his face was obvious, even in the dim, murky light. He cocked his head, peering at me like I was some breed of animal he'd never seen.

I was so flabbergasted to finally have him in front of me that I didn't know what to say, not for a minute or more.

We simply stood there, eyeing each another.

Finally, I said the only thing I could think of, which was stupid but would at least let me know if I was in or out. "Aren't you going to invite me in?"

I expected a smartass reply, but all Boutros did was sigh, turn, and walk away. He'd left the door open, so I took that as an invitation and followed.

As we moved through the apartment, I took note of the carnage—the overflowing ashtrays on the coffee table and bookcases, the stacks of unruly papers scattered across the dining room table, along with Boutros's trusty IBM Selectric (he refused to use a computer to write), the mess of dirty dishes, saucers, cups, and glasses in the kitchen sink and on the counter.

I followed him into his bedroom, which was off the kitchen (sounds weird, but it wasn't uncommon in older Chicago apartment layouts). Wordlessly, I watched him throw back the quilt and sheet and then crawl into bed. He lay back on the pillow, covers pulled up to his neck, his eyes glazed as though he still didn't recognize me.

I expected him to burst into laughter or to at least smile, but no evidence of mirth emerged. He rolled over toward the wall and lay on his side, eyes still open and staring.

Taking a step toward the bed, I asked, "Are you okay? Boutros, tell me you're okay."

He rolled back over on his back and threw back the covers next to him.

I laughed nervously. "You, what, want me to get in bed with you?" Despite having to share a bed on our recent vacation, sharing a bed (or a hug or a kiss for that matter) was simply something we never did.

He said nothing, but he left the covers as they were— an open invitation.

I slid out of my shoes and crawled in with him. I lay back, and he quickly came to me, laying his head on my chest and pulling me closer than I already was. I wrapped one arm around his waist, and with the opposite hand, I stroked his hair.

I didn't know what was wrong. But I wasn't blind. The dark, the mess of the place, his not speaking all added up to his being in a very bad place. I figured he would tell me what happened when he was ready.

We lay like that for a long time, until my eyes grew quite adjusted to the gloom. As my vision cleared, I saw the clothes strewn on the floor and, even here, a couple of dirty plates, an empty pizza box. *At least he's eating*, I thought.

Boutros curled into me, as though he were trying to enter me. Not in a sexual way, mind you, but as though he wanted to vanish into me. Or maybe meld with me, making us one.

It seemed like an hour or more had passed in silence, and maybe it had. I had no gauge. Boutros finally spoke, and when he did, the words he uttered were entirely stripped of the wit and bite I usually associated with him. His voice was a papery croak.

"You've never seen it. Never seen me, not here. But sometimes I go to these dark places, or they come to me. I've never really figured out how it works. But it's like a big, black stain covering me. My mum had the same thing. And I can't get out from under it. I feel so alone."

A big pang of guilt rose up within me. "I'm so sorry I wasn't here."

"Oh, bother. You're here now." He squeezed me.

"I should have checked in. I've been bad."

"What? Checked in? Like I'm an invalid?"

I laughed, but it seemed weird in the dark, in this mood, so I cut it short. "You know what I mean."

"I know. I know you're busy falling in love. I didn't expect you to come around."

"I was worried."

"I know." He moved his head on my chest and paused to plant a little kiss on my cheek.

"I never forgot about you."

"I know." He rolled away, turning over to once again face the wall. "Would you mind staying here, just until I fall asleep?"

"Not at all." I made like a spoon with him, holding him not only until he fell asleep, but I did too.

When morning came, the sunlight streamed in, illuminating the havoc, the mess.

Boutros rolled over, rubbing his eyes. He looked at me as if shocked. "What the hell are you doing here?"

"You asked me to stay."

"Until I fell asleep, my dear. I am not one of your one-night stands."

"And...you're back."

He smiled, but there was a bit of fatigue I hadn't seen before clinging to his features, as though he'd aged a couple of years in the past few days. "Don't you have to go to work?"

"I don't have to. I can stay here. I'll call in." I mock coughed a couple of times.

"If you stay here, I'll put you to work cleaning up this mess. Scratch that, I don't want those hands touching plates I eat off of." He laughed, and this time it sounded like the old Boutros. I was relieved. I was also relieved at being excused from the daunting task of cleaning up the wreckage of his apartment.

"Fine." I threw off the covers and swung my legs out of the bed. "If you're sure you're okay."

"Am I ever okay? Do you know me?"

"Point taken."

I got dressed and headed out. As I reached the front door, Boutros hurried behind me and tapped me on the shoulder. When I turned, his face looked a little panicked.

"Thank you," he said. "You're the only one who sees me."

I nodded. I got it. Now would be a good time to hug, I thought. And I tried.

He shoved me away. "Get out of here."

"I'll call you later. Pick up."

I didn't wait for him to answer. I trotted down the stairs, hoping this dark stranger, whoever or whatever it was, would never return to plague Boutros again.

Well, I could hope.

Chapter Seventeen

"So, this guy in Boston? Is he, like, special?"

I shouldn't have picked up the phone. I needed to get out to O'Hare, and public transportation in Chicago, on a weekday morning, was nothing close to reliable. Plus I lived in freaking Rogers Park, bordered to the east by the lake and to the west...well, a tangle of local streets. There was no fast and easy route out to the airport from where I lived. The best way was simply to take Touhy Avenue west for miles and miles and miles, through several neighborhoods and suburbs and stopping at endless lights.

I needed to get going. My bag was packed. I was dressed. I'd taken AJ over to my friend Camille's the afternoon before. I'd had some scrambled eggs and a cup of coffee. I'd called for a cab, since I didn't want to rely on the CTA.

And then the phone rang.

I stood near my front door, debating. Something, a little presentiment perhaps, told me I should answer it. My mother hadn't been feeling well lately, and she was getting up in years—plus I would not be reachable by phone for the next several hours. It would take me a full day to get to Logan and then out to New Hampshire via bus. Remember, this was a time, albeit recent, before cell phones were in common usage.

So I was compelled to answer, even though I knew my cab would be pulling up outside any minute.

I grabbed the cordless from its stand and headed outside to the balcony, where I could watch for my cab's approach.

It was Tom. We'd had a date last night that had started off wonderfully, burgers and beers at Moody's Pub on Broadway and then back here for the "dessert" neither of us were even beginning to tire of.

I'd put off and put off and put off letting him know about my plans for a long weekend on the East Coast, but last night, because I kind of had to shove him out of bed and send him home, I ran out of excuses.

"Um," I began, in bed and postcoital. Probably not the best time, but I wondered if there really was a best time to let the man you're seeing know you're going off to shack up with another guy for a few days. "I, uh, need you to—" No. What was the best way to tell someone with whom you've been spending lots of nights together that tonight would not be one of those nights? There was no best way. I blurted, "It's, uh, not a good idea for you to stay here tonight." I smiled, and I'm sure it came out looking more like a grimace. "I have to get up early."

"So? We both have to get up early. For work. D'uh." He rolled over and yanked the covers up to his ears. In seconds, he was snoring. Good sex will do that, especially to guys in their twenties, but Tom had an almost superhuman ability to fall asleep at the drop of a hat. I wondered if maybe he didn't have a touch of narcolepsy.

I shook his shoulder. "Honey? I wasn't kidding."

He rolled over and eyed me. I almost reconsidered going in the morning. His topaz eyes made me melt. I was nearly overcome with shame and lust for the guy lying next to me under warm sheets.

"I don't get it. Why can't I stay?"

I sat up and sighed. I groped around on the nightstand to find my smokes. I shook one out and lit it.

"Can I have one?"

I tossed him the pack, and we both smoked in the dark for a while.

"I should have told you this, but—"

"Uh-oh," Tom said.

"No, no, it's nothing bad! I just, uh, neglected to mention that I'm heading out for a few days. No biggie. Slipped my mind."

Tom sat up next to me, our shoulders touching. "Where are you goin'? Can I come?" He pushed against me a little with his shoulder.

"I wish you could! But I planned this trip a while back, before we met."

"Are you going to see another man?" He snorted with laughter.

I shivered. "Well, not exactly." I opted to tell the truth, sort of. "I don't know if you knew this about me, but I always wanted to check out Boston. See, I was accepted by Emerson College back when I graduated high school, and I wanted to go there so, so bad! But in the end, my parents just couldn't afford it. Anyway, when I was over in England, I made the acquaintance of this guy who's from there. Just at one of the bars. He said I could come and check out the city, and I could crash at his place. So I took him up on it. Just to see Boston, you know."

"Okay." Tom sounded dubious. I couldn't blame him. But what could I say? I didn't want to hurt him. I didn't want to jeopardize this magic thing that was beginning to bloom between us.

If it's so magical, I wondered, *why am I running off to Boston?*

The answer to that was that my time with Walt had been magical too. And I needed to see if there was something there.

I was a hot mess and hated myself a little right then.

"I'll just be gone through the weekend. We can meet up as soon as I get home next week. You can stay over then for sure." I touched his shoulder. "I hate to throw you out, baby. You know how much I love to fall asleep all curled up next to you. But I need to get up early. I left all my packing to do in the morning, plus I need to allow plenty of time to get to O'Hare."

Reluctantly, he'd dressed and left, a little morose. But at least he didn't press me about Walt.

Until this morning. Why had I answered the phone?

"So, this guy in Boston? Is he, like, special?"

"He's just a friend," I answered, feeling like a heel. Yes, I suppose Walt was a friend, but he was something more too. The fact that I didn't know quite what—not yet—was just a point for further pondering and exploration.

"You sure?" Tom sounded incredulous, and I certainly couldn't blame him, since I was stretching the truth well past its breaking point.

I skirted the question about my certainty. "Look, it's just for a few days. I'll be home Monday morning. Why don't you plan on coming over after work on Monday? I'll grill us a couple strip steaks and make a big salad. I'll even make an apple pie."

Except what if I came home even more in love with Walt? What if my four days out east turned out to be transformational? What if I saw, at last, that Walt and I *could* make a long-distance romance work?

Would I really want Tom lumbering around my apartment, expecting dinner and sex? Would I feel annoyed with him when he switched on *The Nanny*, at which he'd laugh throughout every episode while I cringed at Fran Drescher's voice?

"You know what?" Tom asked. I could hear the rage simmering beneath his words. "I don't know if I buy your story. So you go off and see your 'friend.' Have a great time and don't even give me a second thought."

He hung up without giving me a chance to say another word.

Wow. I never knew Tom had such a propensity for anger. He was my easygoing, simple, uncomplicated guy, or so I'd thought.

I saw the yellow cab turning from Ashland onto Fargo and went back inside. I had this sick feeling that I was gambling with very high stakes and could come out of this game empty-handed.

Was this trip really worth it?

As I grabbed my suitcase and headed out the door, making sure it was locked behind me, I thought that the question was moot because this trip was already set in motion. No turning back now.

And I argued with myself as I stepped from the vestibule out onto the street, headed toward my waiting taxi. The driver flipped the trunk open when he saw me approach. *You know*, I told myself, *you can do anything you want. You can tell the cabbie to cancel this trip. You can turn around, go back upstairs, and unpack. You can give Tom a call on his morning break at ten and apologize and hope that he'd like to get together tonight.* A pang of longing went through me at the thought, and an image of his smile seized up my heart.

I could do all of these things. The worst that would happen is I'd be out of a great deal of money that I didn't have because my airfare was nonrefundable.

And I'd miss out on seeing Boston.

And Walt. He'd be so disappointed. And so would I.

I got in the cab and told the driver I was headed to O'Hare and flying out on American. I needed to see.

I just needed to see.

*

Walt had emailed me earlier in the week with specific directions on how to get to him at his friend's place in New Hampshire. I was to take the subway, which he called the T, to an area a little north of downtown Boston, where I would pick up a local commuter bus that would take me to within five miles of him.

He'd made arrangements with a friend to pick me up at a general store in the middle of nowhere.

I was nervous because I wasn't accustomed to much travel at all (I'd grown up poor; the only vacations I could recall my family taking were to visit relatives in Michigan), and I sure as hell wasn't accustomed to traveling alone.

But fate or God or good fortune or whatever you want to call it had been with me all morning, starting when I got in the cab. The ride to the airport had the usual delays at busy intersections, but no real traffic snarls. I got to O'Hare with time to spare. The flight was on time and arrived at Logan just when it was supposed to.

The T was easy, thanks to Walt's very specific instructions regarding where to catch it and how to pay for travel on it.

And the bus ride north into New Hampshire was pleasant. It was a perfect sunny day, not a cloud in the sky, the temperature hovering around eighty with no humidity. It calmed me. The gorgeous day, along with the anticipation of seeing Walt again, made the difficult talk I'd had with Tom that morning fade into the background. I smiled, looking forward to things.

As I came up the road to the house, my suitcase rolling along obediently behind, Walt stood in the distance at the screened front door. My heart gave a little leap. Even obscured by the dark mesh, his handsome face, with its sharp planes and bushy mustache, still called to me. I think I'd forgotten how fine it was and how it had an effortless ability to stir both my soul and my loins.

A smile lit up his face as I drew closer.

He opened the door and stepped back a little to admit me.

There were no words. We fell into each other's arms like two long-term lovers, reunited after years apart, which was the story I had playing in my head. When he kissed me deeply, it was magical and electric all at the same time. I tingled everywhere. It was as though I'd been a man dying of thirst in the desert and his kiss was my oasis.

It was definitely not a mirage.

Wordlessly, I followed him inside, our fingers intertwined as we headed up the stairs. He only paused once to say, "I'm so glad you're here. I'll give you the tour later, okay? Right now, there's just one room I want to show you." His voice was husky with desire, and his eyes were alight with lust. I felt a chill. And a tightening in my shorts.

He'd mentioned the room earlier, and I hadn't given it much thought, but now he led me up a narrow set of stairs to a small third floor that was all one room. There was a rough-hewn hardwood plank floor, bare white walls that slanted inward, a couple of nightstands with Tiffany-style cut-glass lamps, and a big brass bed with a white comforter and a mountain of white pillows. A huge skylight illuminated the entire room, flooding it with yellow light. The other two windows faced out toward tree-covered mountains. Here and there were spots of orange, red, and yellow, but not many. Fall was still just an idea so far, a what-if. But the harbingers were out there, biding their time.

We undressed quickly. Walt flung a few pillows to the floor, threw back the comforter and the sheets, and before I knew it, we were on the bed and he was inside me. I'd been playing the top role for so many weeks, I'd almost forgotten the joy of bottoming, especially for a top who knew exactly what he was doing. It didn't take long before, gasping, I witnessed white arcs of come jetting out of me into the buttery light to land on my tanned stomach.

I watched Walt's face, upon seeing this, morph into something that looked like a cross between agony and ecstasy, but I'd lay odds that it was the latter.

After we'd regained our regular respiration and our heartbeats returned to normal, I nudged him.

"What? Ready for round two?"

"Oh, honey, I'm always ready for round two. You should know that by now. But right this moment, I need a couple other things. One, I want a tour of the house, like you promised. It looked amazing in the little glimpse that I got." And it had. From the road, it hadn't looked like much—a white brick ranch house at the top of a hill. But once inside, I realized it was huge and opulent, built into the side of a hill so its grandeur was not immediately apparent. Hidden, really, from casual passersby. "I also need to eat."

Walt hopped off the bed and struggled into his clothes.

"I think we can make both of those things happen. Get dressed. Or not. There's no one to see us out here, so you don't have to get dressed again until, oh, maybe Sunday afternoon, when I have a couple of friends I want you to meet coming over for dinner."

"Oh?"

"Yeah, a brand-new couple. One's a performance artist from New York, the Lower East Side. Maureen. Her latest love is Joanne, who, believe it or not, is an attorney."

I laughed, sliding into my shorts. I didn't know I could be comfortable enough without clothes. I had a weird aversion to sitting on furniture without something between my butt crack and the upholstery, no matter how romantic the idea might be. "Why wouldn't I believe that?"

"I don't know. They're just such opposites. Mo's a free spirit, brilliant, artsy. Out and proud bisexual. You never know what she's gonna say or do next. And Joanne is button-down shirts and Brooks Brothers suits, practical to a fault. Militant feminist. Just very, very different."

The description made me think of Tom. I saw him in my living room, watching *The Fresh Prince of Bel-Air* and chuckling kind of mindlessly, unaware that I was studying him. I remembered him telling me over dinner at a Polish smorgasbord restaurant on Milwaukee Avenue that he never read books and, in fact, had only finished one, *Of Mice and Men*, in high school. Even though I knew it was cruel, I'd wondered if he was my Lenny.

Yet thinking of Tom made me miss him and his simple ways. I also thought of him over me after sex, wiping me down with a warm cloth and looking at me with utter adoration.

We, too, were opposites, but somehow we seemed to work.

"They complement each other," I said, as we headed down the narrow stairs to the main part of the house.

*

The tour revealed a house the likes of which I'd never seen. I mean, I grew up in the poor part of a struggling, seen-better-days, industrial small town in the foothills of the Appalachians. We had two tiny bedrooms and one bathroom for the whole family. Wall-to-wall carpeting was luxury.

This place? I don't even know how to begin describing it. The floors throughout were wide-plank pale wood that, despite their matte finish, rusty nails, and purposeful scuffs, carried about them a kind of simple elegance. The windows were all framed in dark wood and stretched, in almost every instance, from floor to ceiling, revealing sun-dashed forest landscapes of breathtaking scope and beauty. Furnishings were simple, and even a decorating novice like me could tell they were very, very luxurious. Here and there, worn Oriental rugs in reds, grays, creams, and blacks covered areas and defined rooms. Light fixtures were tarnished brass and dark metal, continuing the feel of a cabin. But this was too large to be a cabin. Art graced the walls, huge canvasses, displaying everything from almost photographic realism, to pop art, to impressionism, to abstract expressionism. I had a feeling that most, if not all, of the work was original.

"This is my favorite part," Walt said, leading me outside through a pair of French doors at the rear of the house.

Below me was one of the most gorgeous swimming pools I'd ever seen. It was irregularly shaped, like a pond, and surrounded with boulders and pampas grass. In the middle of it was a small grassy island, which I would guess was about ten by ten. One end of the pool had a cascading waterfall, the water tumbling over ochre and red stones. The pool was lined with small pebbles instead of concrete, and the pale-green water shimmered in the sun. A few lily pads floated on its surface.

"It almost looks like a real pond." Obvious, but it was all I could think to say.

"Enhanced reality." Walt pointed out a little twin of the house next to the pool. "That's the pool house. It's got its own bath, kitchen, and living suite. I'll show it to you later."

I couldn't help but think how this small "spare" house was more luxurious than the home I'd grown up in. It made me excited and a little nauseous all at the same time. All of this opulence was making me feel out of my element, as though I somehow didn't deserve to be here.

I turned to Walt. "Who *is* this friend of yours, anyway?"

He blurted out the unfamiliar name. "You know, the fashion designer."

I shook my head.

"Come on. You probably have some of his labels in your closet back in Chicago."

I doubted it. I did my clothes shopping at TJ Maxx, Target, and the Brown Elephant thrift store on Halsted.

"And you know him how?"

"We went to Princeton together."

I gulped. Why was this conversation suddenly making me so uncomfortable? "You went to Princeton?"

"Yeah, didn't I tell you?"

"On a scholarship?"

Walt looked puzzled and shook his head. "No." He took my hand. "Let me show you the kitchen, and I can make you something to eat." He grinned devilishly. "I want to make sure you keep your stamina up." He stopped and peered over his shoulder, then nodded toward the pool. "See that little island? We can make lots of fun use of that later on."

It took my eyes a moment to adjust to the darkness of the house after the brilliant sunshine. I felt disoriented and a little lost. I'd grown up poor, but not wanting for anything. Dad was a welder, and Mom took care of my sisters and me and our little house. They had a Christmas club at the bank—and beyond that, they pretty much lived paycheck to paycheck. If not for a scholarship and loans, I would have never been able to afford even a state school like Miami University.

Walt started toward the kitchen, blissfully unaware of my conflicted feelings, as far as I could tell.

"Wait." I stood still in my tracks near the French doors.

He turned, cocked his head.

"I didn't know you attended an Ivy League school."

He shrugged. "It never came up. It's no big thing, really. Where did you go?"

"Miami University."

"In Florida?"

I didn't bother to tell him I'd never been to Florida. "No. Small town in Ohio, near Cincinnati."

"Okay." He took a few steps toward the kitchen. "I could make us a big salad. There's a farm stand down the road, and I got some glorious tomatoes and butter lettuce. And I could sear some seitan to put on top. You like seitan? I made it myself."

"I don't know," I mumbled. I didn't know what seitan was. "So, uh, I thought you told me when we were in England that you lived very frugally, that you didn't have much money." *Like me.*

"I do. I try to keep kind of footloose and fancy free, and that means not being tied down by material things. Someone told me once, or maybe I read it, that the more stuff you have, the less free you are."

Spoken like a rich person, I couldn't help but think. I guess it was my own fault for assuming that Walt, with his rent-a-wreck car and his house-share lodgings was just as poor as I was. And I wasn't even poor! Or at least I hadn't felt that way until I'd come here, to this mansion coyly called a cabin, to hook up with this Ivy Leaguer. Why did I feel somehow sullied, somehow deceived?

"So you come from money?" I blurted out.

"I guess. But really, that doesn't matter to me. Money's not important."

Spoken like a person with plenty of the green. See how "not important" money is when you're trying to decide between paying your rent or buying more food for the week. I smiled, but it left a bitter taste in my mouth. "So I guess you get a little help from Mom and Dad? Here and there?" *So those European jaunts aren't quite so grueling.*

Walt stared at me for a moment, eyes narrowed. "Yes, I have a trust fund, if you're wondering. It helps keep me afloat. A little safety net."

"A safety net? Nice." I smiled, but part of me wanted to be alone. I didn't quite get why this was affecting me so. Most of my younger gay friends would be delighted happening on a rich boyfriend. But all I felt was out of my depth.

All I felt was a longing for the simplicity of Tom.

Ah, I told myself, *you're jumping to conclusions. Give the guy a chance. Rich doesn't equal being an asshole.*

"A salad?" I was trying to get back to the subject at hand. "Got any deli meat? A big sandwich sounds amazing. With some of those homegrown tomatoes and that lettuce."

Walt looked at me as though I'd proposed ripping a leg off one of the dining room chairs and gnawing on that. "I don't eat meat. I thought you knew that."

"Baloney!"

"No, there's none of that either."

We paused, stared at each, and then burst into laughter.

For the moment, the tension that hung in the room like mountain fog dispersed. "I don't remember you being a vegetarian." But then, we hadn't shared much food beyond a bun with strawberries and clotted cream.

"Since I was twelve years old I haven't ingested anything with a face."

"Really?"

He nodded and turned back toward the kitchen. "Seitan is kind of like meat. You can slice it up for a sandwich."

"Tastes like chicken?" I followed him, but reluctantly. Where had my appetite gone?

I slept on my own that night, claiming—truthfully—that I was exhausted from my travels.

*

The next day, we did make use of the little island in the middle of the pool. With sunlight streaming down on our backs and water gurgling all around us, Walt took me forcefully from behind. It was not a gentle fuck, and we both could have roused the dead with our cries when we came, almost simultaneously. I swear to God, birds took wing at the racket we made.

It should have been wonderful.

It should have been searing hot, like something out of a Chi Chi LaRue porn video.

But it wasn't.

As I lay gasping on the fake grass, Walt pressed against me, all I felt was guilty—and trapped. And hot— but not in a good way.

I pushed him away and rolled into the water.

I dove deep, to the bottom of the pool's ten-foot depths. The surface underwater looked like river rocks, small ones, dredged up especially to line this very pool. And for all I knew, that may have very well been the case.

Walt had lain too close in the late-afternoon sun and heat, and it made me feel suffocated. I wanted to be away from him.

I swam around underwater until I felt my lungs would burst and then surfaced, treading water far from the little island.

Walt was watching me and smiling as I glanced at him. He gave a little wave.

Like an otter, I dove back under. It felt safe there, like an escape.

When I finally pulled myself up on the island, out of breath and hungry, I told Walt. "Mind if I take a little stroll? How far is it to that general store?"

Walt eyed me. I think he was suspicious, even if he wasn't sure what to be suspicious of. "You want me to go with you?" He sat up.

I waved him away. "That's okay. Just need a little me time." I smiled but couldn't help feeling as though I was behaving like an ungrateful ass.

He nodded slowly. "All right. Yeah, just walk down the road. It's a mile or two at the most. It's pretty. Maybe you can bring back some dessert? They have a lovely apple cobbler. A local woman bakes it fresh every day."

"Sounds good. I'll bring us back some."

I dropped back into the water.

Walt called after me. "You okay?"

I wasn't. Not at all. This wasn't the trip I'd expected. This wasn't what I'd been looking for at all. Back before I'd met Tom, I thought this little jaunt to the East Coast would be magical, a fairy tale in which I would, after kissing way too many frogs, at last find my prince.

As I swam, I looked back over my shoulder at Walt. He was a black silhouette against the sun, so I couldn't discern his expression.

I called out, "I'm okay. No worries!"

When I reached the edge of the pool, I heaved myself out, not bothering with the ladder.

I walked toward the pool house, where we'd left our clothes.

When I headed out for my "me time," I didn't look back at Walt. I was beginning now to feel sorry for him. Yes, a person can feel sorry for someone even when he himself is the cause of that sorrow.

Things were starting to become clear for me about where my heart was.

*

At the general store, I bought the last two pieces of apple crisp, a Bartles & Jaymes wine cooler (their liquor department sucked), and a pack of Marlboro Lights. I went outside where there was a little bench and lit up. I opened the wine cooler, took a long swig, and made a face. I probably hadn't had one of these since I was in college, and it was way too sweet. I'd finish it anyway, because it would bring me a little oblivion.

The cigarette, though, was another story. Smoking brought with it an almost heavenly release, like I was scratching my deepest itch. I knew I wouldn't be able to smoke around Walt. When he saw me light a cigarette for the first time back in Bath, you would have thought I'd lit my face on fire. I worried he'd have a stroke, both from shock and from secondhand smoke.

In short, he'd been *horrified*. "You're a smoker?" he asked, voice rising with indignation on the word "smoker."

I'd exhaled, careful to blow the smoke away from him. I felt like a pariah. "You say that like I'm a serial killer, or worse, a Republican." I tried to laugh, but I'd been on the receiving end of abuse like this before, although not from someone I thought I was falling in love with.

"Well, it *is* killing—yourself." He shook his head and walked away from me. The cigarette had no longer tasted good; the nicotine buzz went up in smoke, so to speak.

I managed not to smoke around him in England, but how long could I pull off that trick here? I knew I should quit, but dammit, I wasn't ready.

There were many, many good reasons not to smoke, but doing it for someone else was not one of them.

Ultimately, to kick any bad habit or addiction, the abstinence had to be primarily for the benefit of the person doing the work.

I finished the cigarette and the sugary wine cooler, trying to shut out any thought or internal debate. It was very quiet, save for the background hum of insects in the trees and birdsong. The sunlight lay in dappled patches on the dusty road and sidewalk. No cars passed by. Because of the humidity, there was a heaviness to the late summer air, but there was also an undercurrent of chill I couldn't ignore. I imagined a New England winter was biding its time just around the corner.

This was only my first day here, and I was already deathly afraid I'd made a mistake in coming. Boutros, always the wiser of the two of us, whispered in my ear. "You're always thinking with your heart, or worse, another organ farther south, instead of using your brain." It was true. My hormones and my heart pretty much ruled when it came to seeking out sex, even companionship and love.

Was I really so different from everyone else?

I didn't know if it was finding out Walt came from money that disturbed me so much. Class difference was a real thing. I never imagined I was afflicted with it, but maybe I was. Maybe I was some sort of reverse snob. Perhaps I identified more strongly with my working-class roots than I realized, and maybe in them I saw things I liked—a certain salt-of-the-earth worldview.

Or it could be that I simply felt Walt had deceived me a little in Europe, coming across as an itinerant traveler, happy-go-lucky and without a care—or a penny—to his name. But I had to allow for the fact that I was simply romanticizing him. Perception is reality, right?

I sighed. I was here now, so I should try to make the most of it. Put on a brave face. Maybe I would surprise myself. Perhaps Walt would surprise me.

It was then I spied the pay phone at the corner of the building. It wasn't a full-fledged booth, more just a phone built into the faded-wood wall, with a ledge beneath it. Beyond that was a trash can.

I threw the wine cooler bottle and cigarettes away and picked up the phone's receiver. Hung it back up. Groped around in my pockets and realized I didn't have change.

Obviously, I needed to get moving and head back to the house where Walt waited. I'd been gone long enough as it was.

I turned and headed back into the store to ask for change from the cashier. See how I listen to my head over my heart?

As I used the old-fashioned dial on the pay phone, I hoped I had successfully remembered Tom's number.

He answered in a couple of rings.

"You're home." I laughed with relief and with the joy that came from hearing his hello.

"Yeah, I called in sick today."

My heart sped up just a bit. "Is everything okay?"

"I'm fine. My car's another story."

Tom drove a red Sentra in a souped-up sports edition. "Oh no! What happened?"

He laughed. "I went out to the Eagle last night and had a few too many. Ended up playing pinball with a few parked cars on Clark."

My stomach dropped, and I didn't know what to say. Red flags popped up around my head the way stars do in cartoons when someone takes a blow to the head.

Red flag number one: *You were out at the Eagle as soon as I left town?* There are probably fifty or more gay bars in Chicago a guy could go to, if a guy simply wanted a drink. I wondered why Tom picked the one that was the most notorious for cruising and its sleazy back room.

Red flag number two: *You were drinking and driving?*

Red flag number three: *You hit a bunch of parked cars...and you're laughing about it?*

I suddenly found that maybe I should have followed my first inclination, which was not to call him. After all, I was visiting another guy, even if I had downplayed the visit to Tom, who obviously wasn't missing me *too* much. I felt twin surges of anger and jealousy.

My thoughts had kept me from speaking long enough for Tom to ask, "You still there?"

"Yeah," I answered, stretching out the word.

"I'm okay," he repeated. "In case you were worried." Until that moment, I wouldn't have guessed Tom was capable of sarcasm.

"I'm glad, really. What made you want to go out on a school night?" I felt a little sick to my stomach. I lit another cigarette.

"I missed you." He laughed. "Why do you ask?" He was quiet for a moment. "Don't tell me you're jealous."

"I'm not," I lied.

"Because if you were, get that thought out of your fuckin' head. I went out because, truly, I missed you and I felt lonely. *Not* horny. Lonely. There's a difference. I played some pool, ran into some guys I knew from the South Side."

I didn't say anything.

"If you're jealous, remember that you left my ass so sore I needed a rest." He laughed.

I didn't. The words just seemed kind of crude, even if they were meant, I'm sure, to be flattering.

I wanted to hang up, but I needed to say something. "I was just thinking about you. Sorry about your car."

"Ah, it's okay. One of those auto body places was in the area—they cruise around looking for accidents—and they were on the scene in, like, minutes. They gave me a sweet deal—towed me right into their shop and said they'd work it so I wouldn't have to pay my deductible."

"What about the cars you hit?"

"Minor stuff. They'll be okay. You park on a busy street like Clark, you gotta expect your car's gonna get damaged sooner or later."

"So you didn't leave a note or anything?"

"Nah. That's what insurance is for."

Wow. Now I really didn't know what to say. We were quiet for several long moments.

"I miss you," Tom said. "How's it going in Boston?"

I didn't want to go into the whole New Hampshire part of the trip. Fortunately for me, and this was so in my favor it made me sort of believe in divine intervention, a recorded voice broke in, telling me I needed to put in more money to continue the call.

"I miss you too. But I gotta go. All out of change!" I had two dollars' worth of quarters in my pocket.

"Okay. Hurry home, Ricky."

The words touched me, in spite of all that had gone on before. "I will," I said, but the connection was already broken.

*

When I got back, I hugged Walt, and then he stepped back, hands on my shoulders. He wriggled his nose. "Have you been smoking?"

I moved back a step so that his hands dropped away. "Come on. Don't ask questions you already know the answer to. You want me to go brush my teeth?"

"Yeah, would you mind? Maybe take a shower?"

"Okay." I rolled my eyes and turned away, then swiveled back to hand him the waxy white paper bag I'd brought. "They had two pieces of the apple crisp left. You're welcome."

He took the sack, and his expression crumpled. "I'm sorry. I didn't mean to be an ass. It's just that I hate to see you harm yourself with those things."

I looked at him with mock surprise. "Don't tell me they're bad for me! I had no idea."

Walt rolled his eyes. "Look, I'll just say this. No smoking in the house. Clean up after yourself and promise me you'll at least think about quitting."

"Okay." I thought about kissing him, then realized the smell would be on my breath and embedded in my hair and mustache. "That shower sounds good anyway. Got all dusty on the walk back. But it *was* pretty."

"You should see it in the fall."

The tension in the air upon my return dissipated pretty quickly. "Well, who knows? Maybe I will."

Walt grinned, and I was reminded of why I'd fallen for him when we were across the pond. He was sexy, sure, but there was something good about him, an inherent kindness that was there if only one would take a moment to look into his eyes.

"Lawrence, the guy who owns this place?"

I nodded.

"He's looking for someone to stay in it through the fall and winter because he'll be in New York and Milan. Not really a caretaker, more of a house sitter. You might want to think about it."

"I have a job." But how cool would it be to quit and come and live here? I could finally finish up that horror novel I'd been writing for years, the one about the serial killer who believed he was a vampire and terrorized Chicago. I imagined being snowed in, rattling around the house, a stew simmering on the stove as snow drifted down outside and a fire crackled in the oversize fieldstone fireplace inside.

"Just give notice at your job. Lawrence will pay you, and you won't have to worry about rent."

"It sounds really tempting." I turned toward the stairs. It did sound tempting—and terribly romantic, in its own way—but pursuing such a route would be a mistake. It was making a too-soon commitment to Walt, in a way. Even though he didn't say it or even hint at, I had a feeling that if I lived here, I'd be isolated, just waiting for him to show up on the weekends.

I also would be leaving behind everything I held dear in Chicago. I loved the city. But more, I loved the people in it. Boutros. And yes, even Tom, despite his drinking and driving. There was still possibility there—he was hugely sexy, even if he was daily proving himself to be about as bright as a ten-watt bulb. But he also had a good heart, and that went a long way with me.

I couldn't really entertain the idea of up and leaving the city I felt was my home.

Besides, quitting would mean more than the loss of a paycheck. It also meant losing my benefits—health insurance was important, so was the little bit I'd built up in my company IRA. Cavalierly quitting a job, I thought, was something someone with a trust fund could afford to do.

I hurried upstairs.

*

When I came back down, freshly showered and shaved, dressed in a pair of comfortable old cutoff jean shorts and my favorite T-shirt, which depicted a caricature of Grace Jones, I could smell something cooking in the kitchen.

I briefly thought about stepping out onto the front porch for a smoke but denied my addiction. I'd promised myself as I scrubbed that I was going to try to make the best of this weekend.

I padded barefoot into the kitchen.

"Hey, good-lookin', what you got cookin'?"

Walt turned from the stove, a wooden spoon in his hand. "Lentil soup. It's from the *Moosewood Cookbook*. You'll love it."

I had to admit that it didn't smell bad. It looked kind of like a bumpy brown slurry, but hey, don't judge, right?

"I'd let you taste it, but it needs another hour to let the flavors marry."

"What's in it? Beef stock?"

"No, silly. It gets its flavor from garlic, herbs, and lots of veggies. Scrumptious! Pull up a stool and grab a glass of wine. It's a nice Syrah."

"Whatever that is." I filled a glass almost to the top.

Walt reached over me to grab the glass before I had a chance to put it to my lips. "That's a glass for white wine." He reached up in the cupboard and brought down a glass that looked more balloon shaped and transferred the wine into it. "There you go. Better bouquet."

I sipped, feeling chastened.

*

Dinner? How do I describe our dinner? Two people alone in the middle of the New England wilderness, in a gorgeous, architecturally significant house could be the perfect setup for romance and intimacy, right? Sure it could.

It could also go the other way. And it did on this night.

It was too silent. The fact that we seemed to suddenly have very little to say to one another made the quiet even more oppressive, as though it were a third presence—a huge third entity that I thought of as a boa constrictor, tightening and tightening around us until neither of us could breathe anymore.

I drank too much wine. I belched midway through the meal and had the nerve to laugh about it while Walt glared at me.

I recalled lamenting to Boutros once that all I wanted was a man I could fart in front of. He got my meaning.

Walt and I did try to make conversation. We really did. But once the soup had been discussed—which was, by the way, delicious—we found we had little more to talk about. Lots and lots needed to be said, I knew, but I don't know if either of us was ready for that conversation.

When we'd finished eating, I said, "You did all the cooking. Why don't you go relax, maybe put on some music, and I'll take care of cleaning up?"

"You don't have to," Walt said. "You're my guest. I'd be happy for the company, though." He lifted my soup bowl and started toward the kitchen.

I jumped up and grabbed the bowl from him. "I insist. I'm not going to let you." I really needed to be alone, so my offer wasn't entirely unselfish. I simply needed some relief from the crushing silence between us.

"You sure?" Walt stood, staring at me. My heart lurched. I could see the sadness in his eyes, sadness I was pretty sure I had inflicted. In the passage of a moment, a mind-movie played, dramatizing Walt's hope and anticipation for this reunion, ending on a discordant note as his disappointment made its first appearance as a dark shadow that grew and grew.

"I'm sorry," I said. "It's the least I can do."

I wouldn't have been surprised if he had countered with "That's for sure," but he had the decency not to.

"I didn't get to meditate today. You're giving me the chance. Go ahead. I'll be out in the pool house if you need to find me." He started out of the room, calling over his shoulder, "I'll put some music on. Any particular stuff you like?"

"Rock, dance," I said, knowing he was probably thinking of something more along the lines of Franz Liszt or Camille Saint-Saens. At least, I was pretty sure that's what he would have chosen.

I grabbed the other bowl and some silverware. The house, predictably, had built-in speakers throughout.

Walt chose the radio—a Top 40 station out of Boston. As I began washing dishes, a song came on that made me cry and made me decide to wash everything by hand to give me more time to think.

The song was Tears for Fears "Mad World." It had always been a song that made me melancholy, with its plaintive longing and minor chords. But tonight, those lyrics about being sad and dreams dying cut straight to my heart.

I plopped down on the marble floor, dishtowel in hand, and sobbed for several minutes. I wanted to go home, sort myself out.

Was being alone such a bad thing?

What had I been doing with my life up to this point? Chasing love through being a slut? I wasn't in my twenties anymore. Had promiscuity ever worked for anyone in terms of finding love, real love? I'd always been sex-positive, but right now I felt like my whole "out" youth, I'd been trading sexual experience for my soul, my future.

Mad world, indeed.

I finished up the dishes and walked to the back door. The pool was a glowing oval from the underwater lighting. A bright, unnatural blue. There was a warm yellow light emanating from the pool house, and I thought of Walt inside, seated on the floor in the lotus position, eyes closed, concentrating on his breath.

I remembered trying to meditate a few times and how I could never calm my monkey mind for more than a few seconds.

Deciding against letting him know I was done with the dishes, I turned and headed up the stairs to bed.

*

I woke in the middle of the night, alone. A crescent moon shone down on me through the skylight. The room glowed with silver light. I glanced over at the empty pillow beside me and wondered if Walt had felt unwelcome, or if maybe he simply couldn't sleep and was up raiding the refrigerator or something.

The pillow looked untouched. He'd never come to bed, at least not with me.

I turned on my back, realizing how odd it was that I'd gone from sleep to wakefulness in a heartbeat. My thoughts assured me that I was done with sleeping for tonight, so I tried to simply relax into the feather pillow beneath me and stare up at the twinkling constellations above. Here, without the light pollution of the city, the sky seemed crowded, a riot of sparkling diamonds.

I longed to talk to Boutros. He'd belittle me. Make fun of me. But in the end, he'd listen like no one else, other than my mother, could. In a left-handed way, he'd let me know that I was worthy of love. He'd remind me to protect my delicate dreamer's heart and that even if I was a "girl of easy virtue," I deserved to find a man who loved me—despite forever going about it the wrong way.

Amazingly, with thoughts of my best friend plus the stars looking down on me, I did manage to fall back asleep that night. I dreamed of a side trip Boutros and I had made when we visited his hometown of Bath, the Glastonbury Tor. He'd wanted to go because he said the tower, and especially the land around it, was a source of powerful spiritual energy going back to King Arthur and having a connection with the Holy Grail. Beneath the tor ran St. Michael's ley line, which Boutros called the "spiritual heart" of Britain. In the dream, I watched him recline across the green, green grass beneath the tor, arms outstretched, to connect with the site's power. I stood back, only watching, afraid to embarrass myself.

*

Morning found me in sun-warmed sheets—still alone. The space on the bed next to me had obviously not been disturbed during the night.

I got up and delayed going downstairs as much as I could. I took a long shower, conditioned my hair, shaved. Took my time figuring out what to wear.

When I came downstairs, I wasn't surprised that Walt was waiting for me. There was no coffee made, no breakfast going. Perhaps I should simply take the day to somehow find my way back to Boston and then home to Chicago.

He sat in a pair of pale-blue boxer shorts on the padded bench seat at the breakfast nook. The morning light shone down on him, making his long hair appear almost red. His skin looked luminous in this light.

But he wasn't smiling. And a big part of me knew I'd brought on the despair I could read on his features.

As I entered the kitchen, he looked up and smiled. Granted, most of the time a smile represents happiness. Yet Walt looked stricken. I wanted to put my arms around him and offer comfort. Yeah, like an arsonist who arrives just in time to put out the fire.

Walt patted the seat next to him. "Ricky. Sit down. We need to talk."

We. Need. To. Talk.

Those words are some of the most dreadful in the English language. I couldn't think of a single time in my own life when they'd been followed by anything other than bad news, condemnation, judgment, or...an ending.

My head told me we were at the end of our road, but my heart, winsome fellow, needed to play it all the way out.

I sat close, my stomach churning. I looked over at Walt, flashing on our memories from England, the thrill of that first night in Brighton.

"Okay, spill it. What's wrong?" he asked.

I went to my go-to default answer. "Nothing. Just still waking up." I rubbed my eyes and then started to rise. "I should make us some coffee. Or do you want tea?" I didn't know.

He took my hand and pulled me gently back down. "Come on. There's something wrong. There's been something wrong since you got here. I have eyes. I'm told I'm a sensitive person. I need to know, Ricky. What is it?"

I shook my head and tried to stop my lower lip from trembling. One thing my whole life I'd been totally shitty at was confrontation. And now I was being forced to play the conflict game—there was no way out. It made me nauseous.

Tom rose up in my mind, his sweet, simple smile. I couldn't imagine anything ever being complicated between us—and that realization cut both ways. But still, it was better than what I had right in front of me, right now.

In a voice barely above a whisper, I said, "There's somebody else. I'm sorry."

"Don't be. And, sweetie, I'm not surprised. It's been pretty obvious you didn't really want to be here."

I wouldn't allow myself to cry. I wanted to, but I needed to save it for later, when I was by myself. I simply needed to get the truth out there, see where it led us.

"I didn't mean for it to happen. I wasn't *looking*. The truth is, I was really excited about getting back together. And then one night, I went into a bar and met Tom." I laughed. "The weird thing is he was nothing like what I thought I would ever seek out." I shrugged. "A blue-collar guy. Not sophisticated in the least. Read one book in his whole life." I turned a little toward Walt, trying to engage his gaze. "But there's something about him. He has a big heart. He's sweet and kind and so, so gentle."

Walt nodded. He picked a piece of lint off his boxers, staring down at the floor. He said, his voice barely above a whisper, "He sounds like a Labrador puppy." He paused for a minute. "That was mean. Forget I said that."

"I don't mean to say *you're* not wonderful, Walt. You are! Handsome, sexy as hell. Fun. Well-read. I think you'll be great—for someone else. I don't even understand why you're not great for me. Isn't the heart strange? Logic tells me to pick you, but my heart is missing Tom."

I stood up. "I need to find out where this thing with Tom is headed. I have to see if it's the real thing, as I suspect it might be." Really? That particular realization was just cementing itself as the words tumbled from my lips unconsidered.

I walked over and peered out the window. The sunlight dappled the tree-covered hills in the distance, and I swear to God, more autumn colors had shown up overnight.

"So...what? You're gonna go home early?"

I hadn't really decided on that, but yeah, now that Walt had uttered the plan, it became apparent that it was the right one, no matter what obstacles might stand in my way.

"Yeah, I think I should. I'll pack my bag and head down the road to the general store. Does that bus run more than once a day?" I could feel a tear brimming at the corner of one eye. I casually brushed it away as though it were an errant crust of sleep.

"Just once a day." Walt's voice was toneless. "But it won't come until two o'clock." He came to stand beside me at the window. "Don't you want to hang out? See Boston? You said you'd never been. You don't have to leave."

I put my hands on his shoulders, forcing myself to meet his eyes. "Yeah, Walt, I do. This was supposed to *be* something, at least for me. And it's not. We both know that. Let's not drag it out."

He turned away. There was no small amount of bitterness in his voice when he said, "Have it your way."

I went upstairs to begin packing.

*

I sat for a long time on the bench in front of the general store. They had a little rack inside with some paperbacks, and I found a copy of a Stephen King book I had yet to read, *Rose Madder*, which had just come out in the paperback version I could afford. The book kept me busy for the several hours I spent waiting for the bus.

It also kept my mind off Walt and off imagining him moping around the house, wondering why it had gone so wrong between us and what he would tell his friends when they arrived.

When I finally got to the airport, I was lucky. Looking back, things like what happened to me that day no longer occur at airports, and it seems oddly quaint. In short, the customer service agent who checked my bag (for free) consulted her screen and told me there was a flight back to Chicago that wasn't full. Would I like a seat on that, since the flight corresponding to my originally booked flight wasn't due to depart until tomorrow?

Of course, I wanted a seat on the flight.

Wonder of wonders, I also had the entire row to myself on a half-empty plane. And, they didn't charge me for the change.

*

When I got home, after the long L ride home from the airport (Blue Line to downtown, Red Line north to Rogers Park), I approached my front door drained: emotionally, physically, and just about in any other way you can think of.

Still, I needed to talk to Tom. I wanted to determine when I could see him again. If I had him figured out, the answer to that timing would be within minutes. As nice and sexy as that prospect seemed, I knew I'd have to put him off until the next day.

The only thing I wanted in my bed that night were my pillows and the comforter I'd picked up on clearance at Marshall's.

Tom picked up on the first ring, and I knew immediately he'd either been snorting coke or crying. His nose sounded completely clogged.

"Hey there! Just wanted to let you know I was home!"

"Already?" he asked in his congested voice. "I thought you had a couple more days out there."

I'd imagined a more excited response to my early return home. "You okay?"

"No."

And I could hear a sob escape him.

"Hey, hey. What's wrong?"

"It's my grandma. She had a heart attack this morning."

"Oh no, Tom! Is she gonna be okay?" I pictured his grandmother, who looked like she weighed little more than eighty pounds.

"She died." And he broke into tears.

"Oh, what can I do?" I knew how much Tom loved the two principal women in his life.

"Can you come over?" His question was so pathetic, so sad, so needy, that I immediately let go of my thoughts of hours and hours of sleep. I looked with longing at my turned-down bed. "Sure. Just let me grab a shower and I'll be right there, okay?"

"Promise me you'll stay all night. I don't want to be alone."

"Yes, yes, of course."

I hung up the phone, undressing as I headed to the shower.

Chapter Eighteen

The next few days passed in a blur. My memory of them is a montage of glimpses, filtered through tear-stained lenses. And, perhaps, filtered through how you can be totally in love with a person and still find him completely exasperating.

Tom desperately needed me. He and his mother hadn't planned for the eventuality of the loss of Tom's grandmother and were at a complete loss as to how to go about planning a wake and a funeral.

I had no such knowledge either, but what I did have was right-mindedness. Once I got Tom and his mom, Linda, to identify a funeral home in Bridgeport, I went about calling and seeing what I could get done over the phone. There wasn't, it turned out, a lot.

Decisions needed to be made. Burial? Cremation? What kind of casket? Budget? Would the deceased be wearing something special of her own or would they like the funeral home to provide attire?

"Sir, you and the family really need to come in so we can make all the right choices for your loved one."

I explained this in Linda's living room. She and Tom huddled in each other's arms on the couch while I, as calmly as I could, laid out what we needed to do, according to the person I'd spoken to at Dawson's Funeral Home.

Tom stared at me as though he didn't recognize me. His eyes were red-rimmed, his mouth half-open. The only thing that stopped him from wiping away snot with the back of his hand was me handing him a paper towel off the kitchen counter. It was like he'd been struck speechless by his grandmother's death. I really felt for him, but dammit, I felt like the burden of planning this funeral was suddenly on my shoulders—and I'd only met the poor woman once.

Linda wasn't much better. She was devastated over losing her mother, which, of course, I could understand and sympathize with. Although I only saw my mom a couple of times a year, we talked at least once a week, usually on Sunday, and I couldn't imagine what the world would be like without her in it. Whenever anything, good or bad, happened to me, my first thought was to call Mom so I could share it with her. I could tear up simply thinking about her being gone.

"I never had to plan anything like this before. I don't think I can do it, Ricky," Tom said. Linda nodded.

I wanted to ask if there wasn't someone else who could help, another family member or a long-term family friend. But I quickly surmised that if there was such a person, he or she would have come forward, would in fact be sitting here with Tom and his mom right now. In addition to or instead of me.

I wanted to cry when I realized how utterly alone Tom and his mom were. He hadn't been kidding when he said that when he was growing up, he and Linda were a kind of you-and-me-against-the-world unit.

I had to help them, so I asked a few questions to get an idea of their budget (not much), what Grandma might wear (a navy-blue dress she'd worn to weddings and funerals for years), and if they wanted her buried or cremated. Since they had no idea or plan of where to bury Grandma, I gently convinced them to consider cremation. "And the best part is, once it's done, you'll have her ashes, so a part of her can be with you always."

This sentiment sent both Tom and Linda into renewed sobs.

But at least I now had enough to go on so that I could go to the funeral home and make some arrangement for them.

I felt good about doing that—like I was suddenly a part of this small, wrecked family.

*

The night before his grandma's combined wake and funeral, Tom lay next to me, sweating and spent, on a horribly uncomfortable sofa bed in Linda's living room. As devastating as his loss was, it hadn't dampened his ardor. We'd just finished round number two.

The room was relatively quiet, other than the steady hum of late-night traffic outside, the occasional roar of a city bus. We'd closed the blinds, but streetlamp light still seeped into the room, throwing orange-yellow slats across the sheet covering us.

In this darkness, Tom whispered, "Grandma was everything to me. Every Saturday when I was a kid, she'd take me downtown on the L. We'd go to Carson Pirie Scott and Marshall Field's. They were both too rich for our blood, or "dear" as she used to say, but she loved to browse, and she usually couldn't help herself so she'd buy me something." I could see his eyes sparkling with tears in the dim light. He swallowed hard.

"There was this one Christmas when I was eight..." his voice trailed off, stopped by his grief. He could barely catch his breath, but I knew he wanted to tell me this story, that it was important that I know. I stroked the hair on his chest and stayed quiet, waiting for him to continue.

"There was this one Christmas I needed a sport coat for our school holiday program. The girls were supposed to wear red dresses and the boys blue sport coats and gray pants. Mom couldn't afford to buy me a sport coat, not even a cheap one at Kmart. She went down to Goodwill and got me this ratty-looking thing. It wasn't even blue. It was black, and the sleeves were like six inches too long. She said I could just roll them up.

"I knew I couldn't ask her to do anything more, but I also knew I'd get teased and bullied if I showed up at school in that jacket. I cried myself to sleep and tried to keep it quiet. Grandma slept in the twin bed across from me, and I know she heard. And I know she understood why I was bawling. But she didn't say anything.

"No, what she did was take me to Marshall Field's the following weekend. And, even though she couldn't afford it, she bought me the most beautiful wool navy-blue blazer she could find. The tailor altered it so it fit perfectly. I was the best-dressed kid in that damn school program."

"That's so sweet. She was kind, your grandma."

"Oh, you don't know the half of it. Like that jacket? She didn't have the money for it. I found out much later, she'd sold the ruby birthstone ring she always wore to our neighbor down the hall to pay for my blazer. She did stuff like that. Took care of us when things were tight, which was a lot."

Tom turned to me. "What am I gonna do without her? I thought I had time to repay her for all her kindnesses to me."

I hugged him. "You're gonna keep her alive." I tapped his chest, right above his heart. "Right here. She'll always be close, always be watching over you like she always has."

We fell asleep that night in each other's arms, Tom in tears and me letting him cry. "Sh" was all I could think to say as I stroked his shoulder, his hair.

I realized that night that sometimes "Sh" was all you needed to say.

*

The funeral, as I said, is now kind of a blur in my memory. I remember how pathetic it was. Linda and Tom, me, a couple of neighbors were all that had shown up.

My heart broke for Tom.

Which is why, at the end of the week of the funeral, we moved in together.

Rash, you're thinking, right? You've only known each other a few weeks. You're yelling, "Act in haste, repent at leisure."

Sometimes you know, though. Sometimes you know when it's right.

Tom needed me.

And I needed to be needed.

So it was a natural fit.

It felt right.

Epilogue

Present Day

So now, Smarty-pants, you're thinking you know how I chose when I was, as the song title says, "Torn Between Two Lovers." Think again, oh smart one.

Tom, right? He wasn't the brightest bulb, but he was good people. And he was sexy—a rugged blue-collar man. You might picture us snuggling in front of the TV for an *I Love Lucy* marathon while the Chicago snow tumbles down outside our apartment window. You might picture us having Sunday dinner at his mom's—pot roasts and mashed potatoes made with cream cheese and butter. You might picture the flame of our lust constantly reigniting and never going out, sort of like the eternal flame at the gravesite of John F. Kennedy in Arlington National Cemetery (or the song by the Bangles).

You can picture a lot of things, can't you?

Or are you thinking Walt? Maybe that I went back and reconsidered, that we had a lot in common, besides an undeniable attraction, and that I came to my senses? That perhaps I took him up on that veiled offer to be a house sitter for that gorgeous place in the wilds of New Hampshire? Maybe we spent a blissful winter there...writing, making love, and eating vegan curry.

Um, no.

Walt and I may have been compatible in many ways, but the fact was, as I quickly discovered, there was no spark between us. No matter how logical a union between us might have seemed, I've learned that a spark needs to be there to kindle love's fire. Sometimes sparks can be wild and unpredictable. And sometimes they can be entirely inappropriate and devoid of logic.

But I believe more in the heart than the head. And a spark, to me, is essential.

Besides, remember when I told you about my contracting hepatitis on my trip to England?

Um, yeah, about that. Walt came down with hepatitis shortly after I flew out of Boston. He made the connection and called me. I didn't deny it. I also won't deny it wasn't a very pleasant conversation. And I won't deny the pesky virus put the final nail in the coffin of our romance.

I never heard from Walt again, save to see his name occasionally in a newspaper or a magazine, writing about some exotic locale or, once, his description of how freeing it was to live in his southern California yurt.

Everything is freeing when you have a trust fund to fall back on.

I'm being bitchy and getting off track.

You want to know who I ended up with, right?

Or you think you know because with Walt gone that left only Tom.

And, for a while, you were right.

It was Tom. After moving in together after his grandmother's funeral, my little one-bedroom apartment on Fargo Avenue quickly became crowded with our stuff and our growing collection of strays, testimony to Tom's kind heart and inability to say no. AJ was joined by two feline sisters, Jeruk and Alani, and then by a dog, Martha Wash, a bulldog mix.

Our apartment also became crowded with another kind of stray, also because of Tom's kind heart and inability to say no, but this time it was to other men.

Lest you want to throw tomatoes at poor Tom for infidelity, know this—we embarked on an open relationship quickly after moving in together. It was a choice we made together. And for a while, it was fun.

But then, like all fun things, it was fun until it wasn't.

And it became a problem not so much because of the other men in our bedroom (and on our living room couch, on our balcony, on our dining room table, and once, memorably, in the basement laundry room of the building), but because of Tom's drinking.

See, Tom was the perfect poster boy for the old recovery saying "One is too many and a thousand is never enough."

I didn't notice right away because I was trying to keep up with him. But after a while, I grew tired of bleary-eyed nauseous mornings and a stranger or two in bed with us.

And I slowed down...and stopped. When we went out, I had club soda or a Coke.

Tom never even noticed my switch. And me, the classic enabler and conflict-avoider, never brought it up.

I simply watched. And counted. And grew more and more frustrated in silence.

So, you see, if you think I chose Tom as my forever man, you were wrong.

Fate took the decision out of my hands. I'd talked endlessly to Boutros about wanting to leave, the conversations usually ending up tearful (on my part) and disgusted (on his) as I wept, "But I love him."

Only a year into our relationship, Tom left me. His departure was via driving into a concrete support for an overpass on his way home from the bars. He died instantly.

He may have fallen asleep at the wheel.

He may have simply swerved erratically, like that night long ago when he told me he'd played pinball with the cars on Clark Street after a night of heavy drinking at the Eagle.

He may have been groping, or being groped by, the young man in the car with him, someone he was perhaps bringing home to share with me, much as a cat drops a dead bird at its beloved owner's front door. Oddly, that young man walked away without a scratch on him.

Whatever the cause, I got woken up by two Chicago police officers at around four o'clock in the morning to learn that my Tom was never coming home.

Now, if you're a little on the heartless side, you might be thinking that I wasn't too broken up. I wanted to leave him, anyway, right?

There was also the fact that none of my friends liked him. Too loud. Too boorish. An embarrassment. Beneath me. My mother couldn't stand him. And I was sick to death of his behavior, especially when drunk.

But you'd be wrong. Tom's death nearly killed me. I felt my grief so acutely that for months after, I'd burst into tears at the slightest memory. I had to move from the apartment we shared. I stayed out of the bars, not because I was no longer drinking, but because they reminded me so much of him.

I thought he left a hole in me that could never be filled again.

I was wrong.

See, during that time of mourning and loss, that time of feeling unmoored and that the world could never be made right again, someone stepped up to comfort me, without expecting anything in return.

Someone who'd always been there for me, my truest and best friend. He'd watched me put on and cast off so many men. He'd nursed me through many a heartbreak and was always my rock and my shoulder to cry on.

And he was there for me when I lost Tom.

He invited me to move into the apartment below him in his building, and together we'd walk along the Chicago River that bordered our neighborhood and we'd talk...and bicker. He made fun of me for my weakness, and he brought me stupid things like cupcakes and Popeyes' fried chicken when I was really low.

He'd made me his mum's best dessert—spotted dick—and joined me in laughing about the custard's unfortunate name.

He took me in when I was high, when I was low, and everywhere in-between.

And I realized the spark had always been there between us, waiting, a warm ember.

*

Now, I'm sitting on our back porch overlooking the river. It's the tail end of autumn, and the trees on the river bank have few of their leaves left, so the riot of colors has dissipated, leaving in their wake barren branches reaching up to the dusky sky like the silhouettes of fingers.

Boutros emerges from the kitchen behind me, bearing two mugs of Typhoo tea, his favorite.

He sits next to me on the vintage glider we found on one of our thrift-store excursions and hands me my mug.

"Did you put sugar in?"

"Three teaspoons," he answers. "I wouldn't want you to fall behind in maintaining that fat ass."

I laugh. "I hate you."

"And I detest you. I'd hate you even more if I thought you were alive."

I put my arm around my Boutros, and he lays his head upon my shoulder. Together, we watch the night descend and the stars come up above us.

And for us.

About the Author

Real Men. True Love.

Rick R. Reed is an award-winning and bestselling author of more than fifty works of published fiction. He is a Lambda Literary Award finalist. *Entertainment Weekly* has described his work as "heartrending and sensitive." *Lambda Literary* has called him: "A writer that doesn't disappoint…" Find him at www.rickrreedreality.blogspot.com. Rick lives in Palm Springs, CA, with his husband, Bruce, and their fierce Chihuahua/Shiba Inu mix, Kodi.

Email: rickrreedbooks@gmail.com

Facebook: www.facebook.com/rickrreedbooks

Twitter: @rickrreed

Website: www.rickrreedreality.blogspot.com

Other NineStar books by this author

Unraveling
Sky Full of Mysteries
The Perils of Intimacy
IM
Chaser
Raining Men
Blue Umbrella Sky
Third Eye
Legally Wed

Hungry for Love
Big Love
A Face without a Heart
Bigger Love

Coming Soon from Rick R. Reed

The Man from Milwaukee

It's the summer of 1991 and serial killer Jeffrey Dahmer has been arrested. His monstrous crimes inspire dread around the globe. But not so much for Emory Hughes, a closeted young man in Chicago, who sees in the cannibal killer a kindred spirit, someone who fights against the dark side of his own nature, as Emory does. He reaches out to Dahmer in prison via letters.

The letters become an escape—from Emory's mother, dying from AIDS, from his uncaring sister, from his dead-end job in downtown Chicago, but most of all, from his own self-hatred.

Dahmer isn't Emory's only lifeline as he begins a tentative relationship with Tyler Kay. He falls for him, and just like Dahmer, wonders how he can get Tyler to *stay*. Emory's desire for love leads him to confront his own grip on reality. For Tyler, the threat of the mild-mannered Emory seems inconsequential, but not taking the threat seriously is at his own peril.

Can Emory discover the roots of his own madness before it's too late and he finds himself following in the footsteps of the man from Milwaukee?

Also Available from NineStar Press

Connect with NineStar Press

www.ninestarpress.com

www.facebook.com/ninestarpress

www.facebook.com/groups/NineStarNiche

www.twitter.com/ninestarpress